ABOUT THE AUTHOR

Susan Price won the Carnegie Medal for *Ghost Drum* in 1987 and was shortlisted again in 1994 for *Head and Tales*. She writes: 'I was born in a slum in Oldbury, West Midlands – no bathroom or running water inside; an outside lavatory shared with several other households; and cockroaches and mice. But we got a council house when I was four, and moved about a mile away, nearer to Dudley, where I still live.

'I have a pet, a little grey tabby cat with white patches. I like sharing my house with another kind of animal. Tig's usually curled up somewhere near me while I'm writing.'

More Supernatural stories, published by Hodder

The Bone-Dog

Susan Price

Hodder
Children's
Books

a division of Hodder Headline plc

Copyright © 1989 Susan Price

First published in Great Britain in 1989
by Scholastic Publications Ltd.
This edition published in 1998
by Hodder Children's Books
a division of Hodder Headline plc
338 Euston Road
London NW1 3BH

A Catalogue record for this book is
available from the British Library

ISBN 0 340 710314

Typeset by Hewer Text Composition Services, Edinburgh
Printed and bound in Great Britain by
Mackays, Chatham, Kent

Chapter One

Her suitcase was too heavy for her mother to carry. A man had had to help her put it up in the rack at Birmingham. Sarah couldn't think how they were going to manage at the other end.

'What are we going to do, Mum? We're too early. Uncle Bryan won't be there.'

'Oh, stop being such a worry!' her mother said.

'But he's expecting us on the next train. He won't be there. We'll have to wait ages and it'll be boring.'

'Your Uncle Bry'll be there, I betcha.'

'How will he? I said we were leaving the house too early. I told you we should catch the next bus. But you wouldn't listen.'

'Oh, stop nagging! Your Uncle Bry'll be there, I tell you. He'll guess. He knew when Tabby died, didn't he?'

'No he didn't,' Sarah said. 'He thought something bad had happened, that's all.'

'Well, it had,' her mother said. 'Tabby had died.'

'But he didn't *know* that. He didn't phone up and say, "Sorry your cat's died," did he? And it was Nana who phoned anyway, not Uncle Bryan; and she said, "Is one of you hurt, 'cos I've had a bad feeling all day" – she didn't know it was Tabby.'

'Well, I think she was doing well to have even guessed that much. And remember not to call her "Nana". She doesn't like it.'

Sarah sat back sulkily on the train seat, and its cover prickled her legs. She quite liked going to stay with Gran Gornal, sometimes. At other times – like now – she didn't really want to go much, but everyone took it for granted that she did and it was hard to disappoint them. It was the little things that made it such a nuisance, like remembering that her father's mother always had to be called 'Nana' because she hated being called 'Granny', but that if she called her mother's mother 'Nana', then Gran Gornal would get angry and say, 'A nanny's a paid servant, and I'm nobody's servant and don't you forget it!'

Sarah looked out of the window, watching everything whizz past in grey streaks. 'What's the station we've got to get off at, Mum?'

'Sandwell and Dudley.'

'I'll keep an eye out for it.' Sarah applied her forehead to the window of the train and stared out so that she shouldn't miss a thing, let alone the station.

Her mother sighed, closed her eyes and smiled. 'We won't miss it, Sarah.'

'Maybe we should, because Uncle Bryan's not going to be there. We're too early. By the time we've missed our station and come back to the right one again he will be there, so it's best if we do miss it, really.'

'Stop looking for it then. Honestly, I shall be glad to get back to a quiet house without you. Rattle, rattle, like a pebble in a can.'

Sarah took her head from the window and looked at her mother. 'That's a terrible thing to say about your own daughter.'

'My daughter can be a terrible thing.'

Sarah put her forehead back on the window. 'I can see why you want me to go and stop with Granny Gornal now.'

'Don't you want to stop with your granny?' Sarah, sulking, didn't answer. 'Sarah? Don't you want to stop? Why didn't you say? If you don't want to stay then we can just visit and you can come home with me. Your granny won't mind.'

Sarah immediately and completely changed her mind. She had been thinking that she didn't want to stay with her gran, but now that it seemed likely she'd be taken home again, she suddenly realized how much better staying with her gran was than being at home. Her parents wouldn't let her stay up until she was falling asleep in her chair. They always made her go to bed hours before she was tired and she had to lie awake, bored. And her parents wouldn't bring her home bottles of bubble-stuff, as Uncle Bry did. They weren't as interesting as Uncle Bry either. He knew all sorts of people who owned animals. He knew a man who kept pigs and a horse, and hundreds of people who kept dogs and cats, and even some who kept snakes and spiders. He went around visiting them all, and when she stayed with her gran he took her with him. Last year he'd taken her to the house of a woman who had foxes in her garden, and they'd all sat at the window of an upstairs room, drinking hot chocolate and watching the foxes come running through the dusk to the food put out for them.

'No, I'll stay with Granny,' she said, with a heavy, martyred sigh. 'Granny expects me to. She'll be disappointed if I don't.'

'I don't want you to stay if you're going to be miserable. Your gran won't like that.'

Sarah sighed deeply. 'I won't be miserable. But it wouldn't be fair not to stay now Gran's gone and bought coco-pops and animal biscuits for me.'

'Oh, I daresay our Bry can choke the coco-pops and biscuits down,' her mother said. 'No, I think you should come home with me, definitely. I shouldn't be able to sleep, thinking of you crying into your coco-pops.'

Now her mother was teasing. It was something she had in common with her brother, Bryan. Neither of them could resist teasing. Sarah kept her eyes on the factories whizzing past on the other side of the grimy glass, and didn't bite. It was one of the first things you had to learn when your family was full of teasers – don't bite. Just ignore them. Then they get bored and give up.

Sandwell was a small town station. Mrs White got the case down from the rack all by herself. As they went along the narrow aisle, Sarah tried to hold the handle too and help, but only got snapped at by her mother for getting in the way.

'All right, carry it yourself!' Sarah said under her breath. 'Go on, rupture yourself! I don't care.'

They battled through the heavy carriage-door, which kept trying to slide shut, and through the cramped little vestibule, and almost fell through the door on to the platform. Mrs White heaved the case, with swings of her arm, across the platform to a space where it wasn't so crowded.

Sarah was looking up and down the platform, pushing between the people and dodging round them to see better, trying to spot Uncle Bryan. 'You see? He's not here,' she said. 'I told you!'

But she was talking to air. Her mother was gone. She spotted her staggering through the door of the station-building, struggling with the large, heavy case, and quickly ran after her, crossing hard, shiny tiles towards a chrome barrier with turnstiles. A young man, with dark, curly hair like her mother's, reached over the barrier and took the case from her, pulling it through between the bars.

'Here's your Uncle Bryan,' her mother said as she came up. 'I told you he'd be here.'

'It's just a coincidence,' Sarah said.

'Coincidence!' Bryan said. He had a stronger accent than her mother – a deeper, slower way of speaking altogether. 'I got up out of a comfortable bed to come here and carry your bag, Madam.'

'Her's been bothered all the way here that you wouldn't meet us because we'm on an earlier

5

train than the one I said we'd come on,' Mrs White said.

'Oh, that,' Bryan said. 'I guessed you'd be coming early.' He led the way out of the station, heading for the bus stop.

'How did you guess?' Sarah asked.

He shrugged his shoulders. 'Just did.'

'But how?' Sarah insisted. 'How did you know? We didn't tell you. We said we wouldn't be here until eleven o'clock. So how did you know we'd be here now?'

'I don't know. Just did.'

'Just like her father,' Mrs White said. 'Always got to know everything.'

'I guessed,' Bryan said. 'I woke up this morning and it just come into my head: "Bet Our She'll come early." So I come early.'

'Fancy coming all this way just because of that!' Sarah said. 'What if you'd come all this way and we'd come at eleven o'clock like we said we would? You'd be stuck here waiting then, wouldn't you?'

'But you didn't come at eleven o'clock, did you?' Bryan said patiently. 'You came now, and here I am.'

'But you didn't *know* we'd be here!' Sarah, in the excitement of the argument, began to hop and skip as she walked beside him.

'I *did* know. I *guessed*.'

'But guessing isn't—' Sarah broke off and became thoughtful. She dodged behind Bryan and to his other side, where her mother was. 'Mum, is that what you call second sight? I mean, Uncle Bryan knowing we'd be coming early – is that second sight?'

'I suppose you could call it second sight. I don't know what else you'd call it.'

'Call it guessing,' Bryan said.

'Is that like you told me about Gran Gornal in the war?' Sarah said. 'When Gran knew the bomb was going to fall in the street and it did? That was second sight, you said. Knowing things before they're going to happen. Has Uncle Bryan got second sight as well?'

'Why don't you ask him?'

'Have you got second sight, Uncle Bryan?'

'I got double vision,' he said. 'Too much to drink last night.'

'But have you got second sight?'

'Do you mean have I got four eyes?'

'Oh, it's no use talking to you!' Sarah said, leaving him again to walk beside her mother. 'You won't answer anybody properly!'

Bryan and her mother laughed, which made Sarah feel left out and mutinous. She wondered what kind of mood Gran Gornal would be in. In books and films grannies were always cuddly and sweet, scented with lavender and handing out freshly baked cakes. Neither of her grans were at all like that and Sarah wondered sometimes why they weren't, and sometimes why books and films told such lies. Nana White was a teacher and wore tracksuits around her house, and gardened, so you couldn't play in her garden. She was tall and bony and never made cakes

7

or bought them either, because she believed white sugar was poison and a healthy diet was important. She always wore a scent called 'sandalwood' which she bought from the Body Shop.

Gran Gornal was small and plump as grannies were supposed to be, but she was always rather serious and grim and often downright bad tempered. She usually wore a nylon overall in pink or blue checks, and her fingernails were usually dirty. She always had a malty smell hanging about her, like the smell from pub doorways, but it wasn't beer. It was the smell of the 'suds' that lubricated the machinery at the factory where she worked, making screws. She often had lumps of twisted metal called 'swarf' stuck in her fingers, and she would dig them out with a needle. She didn't care what you did in her garden, though, because she just let it grow wild, and she always cooked things like egg and chips, sausage and chips, bacon, tomatoes and chips, fish-fingers and chips, and chip sandwiches, which she called 'chip pieces'.

Sarah preferred Gran Gornal to Nana White, because Gran Gornal's bad temper made her feel at home. Nana White was always polite even when she was furious with you, but you knew where you were with Gran Gornal, who didn't bother to be polite to children. She couldn't ever imagine herself spending the summer holidays with Nana White – not that Nana White would ever have asked her to stay. Both of them would have been driven up the wall in a fortnight.

Uncle Bryan, Mrs White and Sarah caught the bus outside the station. Apart from a short argument between her mother and Bryan over who should pay the fare – Bryan did in the end – they didn't speak to each other during the long ride. The bus made too much noise as it growled and ground over hump-backed canal bridges, up steep hills, and along dark canyons formed by factory walls. Sarah kept twisting and turning to look through the windows, noticing again the differences between this place and her home. She lived on a neat, new estate of little houses with big windows, all built of clean, pale orange bricks. The bricks of these houses were a much angrier, darker red, their corners blunted by age and wear, and all grimed over. The pavements seemed made of brick too – a dark blue brick, almost black. The houses were strung along the streets in long rows – small houses with doors that looked tiny. Every now and then there'd be one boarded up, or blocked up with sheets of corrugated iron. It all looked very old fashioned.

Over a bridge, with a shock that left her stomach behind, she could see the black-green water of the canal, with more dirty factories on either side: factories that seemed badly repaired, patched with corrugated iron, grown up to the doors with tall weeds. Then they were over the bridge and among more factories, passing a garage selling used cars, and then more houses.

It was all very ugly and the sight made Sarah feel depressed. But even while she hated the ugliness she liked it too. She knew it so well, because every year she stayed with her gran. It was a warm, familiar ugliness. If the concrete and the bricks and the scrap iron covered a lot of ground, well, there were flowers filling factory yards, growing through discarded tyres and even in the streets. There were railway embankments so overgrown that they were impassable, and foxes in gardens, and kestrels and, at night, you could look over valleys crammed with thousands and thousands of brilliant coloured lights.

Once they got off the bus at their stop, it was only a few metres to Gran Gornal's. The pavement was of dark blue Staffordshire Blue Bricks. The houses were built in one long line, and after every two houses there was a long, damp, chill alleyway leading to the yard at the back. There were no front gardens or front doors. The doors to the houses were halfway down the alleys – or 'entries' as Bryan and Gran Gornal always called them.

Sarah had always liked the entries. A little groove ran down the middle to carry away the rain-water, but there were always pools of water, and moss grew up the walls. There was a sound of water dripping, and a dank, damp smell. The long, dank, echoing tunnel made her think of castles, though Number 142 Malt Mill Lane was the smallest castle ever.

Bryan unlocked the door and then banged it open with the suitcase he held. The door took them straight into the living-room of the house, and Sarah coughed at the smell of fried food and damp.

Gran Gornal came in from the back room, wearing

her pink checked nylon overall. 'Oh, so you'm here!' she said.

'We copped the earlier train,' Mrs White said.

'He said you had,' Gran Gornal nodded at Bryan. 'You want a cup of tea?'

'I do,' Mrs White said, with feeling.

She went into the kitchen with Gran Gornal. Bryan put the suitcase down and followed them. Everyone had become rather shy and uneasy since coming into the house. It was always like that at the start of the holidays. Afterwards, when her mother had gone home, it would be better. Gran Gornal would become friendlier.

Sarah, left alone in the front room, stood still, absorbing the strangeness of her gran's house. By the end of the holidays she would have grown used to it, and it would seem as ordinary and dull as her own house, but now the strangeness was still fresh. The house sounded different. It was old, and it seemed to sigh and groan to itself if you listened carefully. Whenever you were quiet you could hear a faint, eerie humming, like the sound a cracked cup makes – and there was the constant crooning noise of the traffic going by outside. The house smelled most of fried food, but there was another smell: a musty, slightly sour, somewhat sharp smell which she knew was made by the bundles of leaves that her uncle and gran hung up to dry in lots of different places. It made a change from the smell of coffee and fly-spray, which she always smelled when she came home from school to her own house.

The voices of her gran, mother and uncle buzzed gently from the kitchen. They were in there and couldn't see her, and she was in here, alone. No one to tell what she did. She went a bit wild: sprang into the air and came down on the settee, bounced up and down on it as if it were a trampoline. If her mother or gran knew what she was doing, she would be in trouble. They always said that she would damage the furniture by bouncing on it, but she never had. Anyone could see that it was just the same as it had always been.

She stopped bouncing when she was out of breath, and lay on the settee wondering what to do next. She didn't want to go into the kitchen, so she let herself out of the door and into the entry. She ran down the damp tunnel of soft, crumbling brick and into the yard behind the house.

The yard was very ugly. Close to the house was a small square area of greyish-yellow concrete, that always seemed covered by a layer of dust. Beyond that was a long, narrow strip of garden – a very depressing garden of drab brown soil, full of a lot of boring, leafy plants with very few flowers, all tangled together and overgrown.

It didn't look the way a garden should. Right down the middle was a thin path made of bricks, and dividing the garden from the neighbours' on either side were tottering fences of chestnut palings. The very sight of these thin, grey sticks, barely being held up by the twists of rusty wire, made Sarah want to sit down and put her head in her hands. They

12

were so ugly that they hurt. But at the far end of the garden was what her gran and Bryan called 'the bank', and spilling down from the bank came great waves of greenery. Hawthorn bushes. In spring they foamed with white blossom. If you crept under their branches, you found a dirt path leading up the bank. If you followed it, you left the garden altogether and came into a patch of waste ground, grown over thickly with bushes, trees and weeds. It wasn't a large patch of ground – if you scrambled a little further up the hill, you came to more houses. But while you were on the bank you were so surrounded by trees and tall grass that you couldn't see any houses at all.

Sarah went on a tour of the patch of ground. It was much longer than it was wide – it ran behind all the houses in that street. There was the elder tree, which still had its polka-dot bunches of creamy-greenish flowers. Its leaves were covered with a film of dust and grime and its flowers looked dirty too, like bunches of old, yellowed, grimy lace. She stood looking at the elder for a while, tugging at one of its bunches of flowers but not picking it. Bryan had told her that you should never pick anything from an elder without asking its permission first and its forgiveness afterwards, and that made her wary about picking anything from it, because how could you tell if a tree gave you permission or forgave you?

The may blossom had mostly gone from the hawthorns. May blossom was very beautiful, like foam or cream from a distance, but when you looked at it closely the foam divided into hundreds of small, perfect flowers; and the more you looked at them, the more and more tiny details you could see, until you felt dizzy. But may smelled of death. Bryan said so. That was why you should never take may blossom into a house, he said, because you took the smell of death in with it, and that was bad luck. May blossom sheds its petals in hours when it's cut and taken inside, and that was bad luck too. You'd killed the may by cutting it, and it would have its revenge. Sarah never picked may blossom. It was safer to admire it on the tree.

She left the hawthorn and visited all the brambles that grew around the edges of the wild place. There were berries, but none of them were ripe yet. They would be before she went home, and that would be long before 30 September when the Devil flew over and spat on all the blackberries to mark them as his own; and anyone who touched what belonged to the Devil became the Devil's. Bryan had told her that too.

There was another date, when all the nuts left on the hazel trees became the Devil's and shouldn't be picked. If you went picking them after that date a stranger came along and helped you, and that stranger was the Devil. Sarah couldn't remember the nut-date, so she never picked nuts at all. She wondered if the nuts her mother bought from shops had been picked before they became the Devil's property – though of course it was probably just a story. That's what her father would say – just a story. There was no Devil, her father said. But Sarah wondered if there might not be *something* – not a Devil, perhaps, with horns and a tail, but *something* that it was better not to annoy. If there wasn't, why should Bryan tell her there was, so seriously? But it was often difficult to tell whether Bryan was telling the truth or just making it all up.

She came to the edge of the wild place and peered from among the hawthorns at the yards of the newer houses beyond, pretending that she was a Red Indian peering at the houses of the settlers. Did the people in those houses know that they were being watched? Could they feel the eyes staring from the forest gloom? Did they sense the danger near? Sarah herself nearly jumped from her shoes at a slight movement near her – a man had come up quietly behind her and had crouched down beside her.

'It's only me, bab,' Bryan said, smiling. 'I come to fetch you. Your mum's going in a minute.'

Sarah knew that she was expected to go and say goodbye to her mother. She would much rather not. It was always so embarrassing and awkward. She always just wanted her mother to go, so she could have a good time; but you could never say that.

They went back to the house together, ducking under the hawthorns and scrambling down from the bank into Gran Gornal's garden again.

'There you are,' Mrs White said as they went into the kitchen. 'Oh, you've got yourself so dirty. What have you been doing?'

'Leave her alone. Bit of dirt never hurt nobody,' Gran Gornal said.

'You're a mucky pup,' Mrs White said. 'I'm going now. Going to give me a kiss?'

'Do I have to?' Sarah asked. Bryan laughed, but Gran Gornal said, 'Give your mother a kiss, you little monkey!'

So Sarah kissed her mother's cheek, which instead of being porridge white and porridge textured, as usual, was smooth and coloured and scented with make-up, in honour of the train-journey.

'Now you be good. Behave yourself. I've told your gran to give you a good hiding if you play her up.'

Gran Gornal didn't need to be told, Sarah thought. She wasn't like Nana White. Gran Gornal had been known to clip the ears of children who weren't related to her at all, if they annoyed her. Sarah had once sprayed her Gran Gornal with water from a water-pistol, in the belief that she would get away with it, because only her mum or dad could smack her. She had never completely recovered from the shock of Gran Gornal not only becoming furious, but soundly smacking her legs. And then there had been the further shock of finding that her mother and father weren't at all angry with Gran Gornal for doing so. 'Serves you right, you naughty girl!' her father had said. Ever since, Sarah had always tried to be good while Gran Gornal was around.

'I'll see you on the bus,' Bryan said. 'Just let me finish this cup of tea.'

'We'll go on ahead,' Mrs White said, which meant she had something to say to Sarah in private. She dragged Sarah out of the house by the hand. On their short walk to the bus stop, Mrs White told Sarah, shaking her arm to emphasize the importance of her words, 'Don't keep asking for things; don't ask for spending money; don't ask to go places – you hear me?'

'I never do!' Sarah said. Every year her mother told her this.

'They haven't got a lot of money, and they won't have anything for your keep – here, you're to have this from me and your dad.' She took a five-pound note from her pocket and gave it to Sarah.

'Five pounds!'

'It's got to last you all the time you're here. I don't want you asking Mum or Bryan for anything.'

'I don't ask them – they just give me things.'

'Well, if they give, that's all right. But don't you ask.'

'I wouldn't, Mother! Honest!'

Their conversation ended as Bryan came running after them. 'Hey,' he said, 'do you want a kitten now your cat's dead? I know a woman's got loads of cats. Could get you a kitten easy.'

Sarah turned to her mother abruptly and stared at her.

'Oh, trust you, Bryan!' Mrs White said.

'What have I done?'

'I've just managed to explain to her why we can't have another cat, and you ask do we want a kitten? We just can't afford to keep another cat – nor a dog! They're too much to feed and we can't afford the vet's bills, and that's that, Sarah!'

'I never said anything!' Sarah protested.

'No, but you looked, and before you start the answer's no!'

There was a silence. Then Bryan said, 'Well! What do you think of the weather lately?'

'It's all right for you,' Mrs White said angrily. 'You don't have to pay rent and buy kids' clothes and kids' shoes, and find money for birthdays and Christmas, let alone vets' bills and cat food . . . I'd love a cat! I love cats! But we just don't have the money.'

'Sorry!' Bryan said. 'I'll never mention cats again, promise. Cross me heart, hope not to die. The bus's coming!'

'Now you be *good*!' Mrs White said fiercely, and turned to face the bus.

When they had seen Mrs White onto the bus, and had waved to her as it drove away, they went into the newsagents. Bryan bought an evening paper, and two comics for Sarah. 'You can come with me when I go round,' he said. 'You'll see puppies and kittens and all sorts. I know a bloke keeps tarantulas.'

'I know,' Sarah said. 'We went to see him last year.'

'Oh, yeah,' Bryan said, nodding.

'I wish we *could* have another cat,' Sarah said. 'I used to like having Tabby. She used to sleep on my bed. She used to sit on the wall and wait for me to come home from school. I really loved her.'

'I know how it is,' Bryan said sympathetically. 'Still, if you can't afford it, you can't afford it.

I suppose it's your dad that took her to the vet, wasn't it?'

Sarah looked up at him, puzzled.

'Your mum could have healed 'em without a vet,' Bryan said. 'But your dad don't believe in it, does he?'

'Believe in what?'

'Healing,' Bryan said.

Sarah screwed up her nose. 'What's healing?'

'Healing. Curing. Making things better when they'm bad.'

'Like a doctor?' Sarah said.

'A bit like a doctor, yeah.'

'My mum's not a doctor.'

'Neither am I! Neither's your gran. You don't have to be a doctor to heal.'

'Is that what you do, then? Heal?'

'Yes!' Bryan said in surprise, looking down at her. 'Didn't you know?'

'No,' Sarah said. She'd known that he went to visit a lot of people who all kept animals of one kind or another, and that the animals were usually old or sick . . . 'You heal animals?' she said.

'That's right.' They turned into the damp entry and Bryan opened the door with his key. 'Here you are, Mum; her's all yours,' he shouted. 'You can get that big stick out the pantry and beat her now. Her mother's gone.'

'I'll beat *you*!' Gran Gornal said.

Now that Mrs White had gone, Gran Gornal and Bryan both relaxed. Gran made another pot of tea and sat at the table with Bryan while he looked through the paper. Sarah went out by the back door and returned to her exploration of the bank, coming back from time to time to check on what they were doing. Gran Gornal made egg and chips for their tea, and Sarah was allowed to make a greasy chip-butty, spreading the bread with margarine so that the hot chips would melt it. She enjoyed it more than she'd enjoyed anything for ages. Then she and Gran Gornal went into the other room to watch the children's programmes on the television. Bryan went out somewhere – they didn't ask him where.

'Gran, is Uncle Bryan a vet?'

'A vet? He ain't.'

'But he gives animals tablets and injections.'

'He don't give animals injections. Where'd you get that idea?'

It was true that she had never seen Bryan inject an animal or heard him say that he did. It was thinking of vets that put the idea into her head. 'He gives them tablets though.'

'Oh ar, tablets and powders and things. He does that.'

'Well, that makes him a vet then, doesn't it?'

'No. Vets go to college and all sorts. Bryan's never been to college. He just doctors animals like I used to, like his dad and grandad used to. It runs in the family. . . . They had used to say that my great-grandfather – that'd be your great-great-grandfather – was a witch.'

Sarah twisted round on the floor where she sat to look up at her gran. 'A witch? A man?'

'Men can be witches too.'

'Oh, that's rubbish!' Sarah said. 'There's no such things as witches.'

'Oh, isn't there?' Gran Gornal said, and got up from her chair and went into the kitchen to do the washing-up.

Sarah sat on her own in the front room for a while, but then the quiet and curiosity became too much. She went into the kitchen, leaned against the sink and said, 'How could Great-Great-Grandad be a witch?'

'I don't know how he *could*. He just was.'

'But what did he do that made him a witch?'

'Oh, he made medicines for belly-aches and rashes. And shampoos and stuff for freckles – things like that. And drawing ointment.'

'Drawing ointment?' Sarah said, thinking of a tube of Germolene with a pencil.

'That's for boils. You put it on a boil and it gets hot and draws the poison out. My mum used to make a lot of that – black, sticky stuff it is. My mum was a witch too.'

'Sounds more like a doctor,' Sarah said.

'A sort of doctor. The kind of doctor people go to when they can't afford real doctors. 'Cos when I was a little girl we had to pay the doctor, y'know, and we couldn't afford to. People was hard up in them days. So we used to make our own medicine, and people used to come and buy medicine off us

– for themselves and for their animals. But your great-great-grandad – he was a *real* witch.'

'What did he do?' Sarah asked. 'He couldn't do real magic, could he?'

'I don't know so much,' Gran Gornal said. 'One story they tell about him was about how a farmer came to see him because somebody was stealing the corn that should have been fed to his animals. As soon as Old Devil Gornal seen him, before the farmer even opened his mouth, he says, "The man who saddled your horse this morning's the one that's stealing the corn." And the farmer went back home and kept a watch on the man who'd saddled his horse, and caught him red-handed.'

'But how did he know?' Sarah asked. 'How could he?'

'Well, I can't tell you that. If you don't know I can't tell you. Now, when I was a young girl I used to work in a factory called "Huberts" because it was owned by a family named Huberts. Very rich the Huberts were. One day Mrs Huberts come into the works for some reason, and then the story started going round that she'd lost her ring, a very expensive ring with diamonds and emeralds. If anybody found it they was to bring it to the office and there'd be a reward, you see. Well, as soon as I heard that I just knew where that ring was. I just knew. I couldn't go on working, not for a second. I just had to leave that machine and go – out into the yard, straight to where I knew the ring was. I picked it up out of a puddle, all muddy it was, just inside the entrance. Lying in amongst the cobbles, all slushy and mucky – nobody would have noticed it. It was all covered in dirt. But I went straight to it, like I was being pulled along on a string. I took it to the office and Mr Huberts gave me a pound. That was a lot of money then, but it wasn't much compared to what the ring was worth. Old Devil Gornal would have done better than a pound, I'll tell you!'

'He'd have turned Mr Huberts into a frog!' Sarah said, and Gran Gornal laughed. Sarah swung herself from side to side, feeling proud. It wasn't easy to make Gran Gornal laugh. 'But what does it feel like, Gran, to know something like that? How did you know you wasn't just imagining where the ring was? How did you know it'd really be there?'

'If you don't know, I can't tell you. There's just no mistaking the feeling when it comes. Sometimes you fool yourself. If there's something you want to happen very bad, sometimes you fool yourself that you *know* it's going to happen, and then you're disappointed. But when it's the real thing, it's like you've been hit with something. It's stronger, much stronger than when you're just imagining it. When I knew where that ring was, it was as if somebody had got hold of me and was dragging me away from that machine to go and fetch it. Dragging me and pushing me towards where it was. And when I knowed the bomb was going to fall, I *knowed* it; I could feel something pushing me away from where the bomb was going to drop. And it's like something's sitting on your shoulders or hanging over you. It's a *feeling*.'

23

'Oh, sounds spooky!' Sarah said. 'Gran? Do you think I might have it?'

'Oh, I dunno. You're only a half a Gornal and your dad don't believe in nothing like that, does he? Because it isn't in his family, see, so he don't believe it. He thinks we make it all up, don't he?' Sarah didn't answer. 'I know he does,' Gran Gornal said. 'He don't like you coming here, does he? Thinks we'm a bad influence.'

Sarah wondered how her gran knew. She was much too polite to admit that she had heard her father say some very rude things about her Gran Gornal and Uncle Bryan. Instead she said, 'But Bryan's got second sight and he's only half a Gornal.'

'Oh no,' her gran said. 'Because I was a Gornal before I married, and I married a Gornal as well – he was my second cousin. So Bryan's got it from both sides. Mind you, your mother has as well and her's never showed much sign of it.'

'So I won't be able to know things like that?' Sarah said.

'Oh, I don't know as it's a gift much worth having,' Gran Gornal said. 'You be clever and get on in the world like your dad. Make a lot of money – that's what makes the world go round. There's none of the Gornals ever been much good at making money except for Old Devil Gornal, and he spent it or gave it away as soon as he made it.'

'I'd rather know things like you and Bryan than make a lot of money,' Sarah said.

Gran Gornal laughed. 'Ar, that's what you

think now. You'll change your mind before you're much older.'

Sarah didn't like being told that she would change her mind, and went back into the other room and read the comics Bryan had bought her.

Bryan didn't come home until mid-evening. When Gran Gornal opened the door for him he came in carrying a large cardboard box. Grinning at Sarah, he said, 'Have a guess what's in here!'

But a squeak from inside the box told Sarah before she had to guess. 'Kittens!'

Bryan knelt on the hearth and unfolded the top of the box. Sarah had thrown herself down beside it, so she could see inside as soon as it was open. Four kittens – three black and white and one tabby. Tiny bumbling little round things, with little pointed tails. She reached in to lift the tabby one out. It was so soft and so light that she could hardly feel it in her hands.

'They're all spoken for, mind,' Bryan said. 'They're only here for tonight. I've got to take 'em to their new homes tomorrow.'

'Oh, I wish I could keep one,' Sarah said. 'I can't have one at home, but I could have one here, couldn't I? I'd pay for it with my pocket-money and—'

'Ask your gran,' Bryan said.

Sarah turned to her grandmother, but before she could speak, Gran Gornal said, 'You needn't think it! I'm having no cats here, nor no dogs or budgies or tarantuling spiders nor nothing else. I'm past the age of looking after other people's animals.'

Bryan was sitting back on his heels, watching Sarah stroke the kitten in her lap. His face was unusually serious and thoughtful. 'Put the kettle on, our mother,' he said, and watched his mother leave the room.

When the kitchen door was closed, he leaned over to Sarah and said quietly, 'Would you really like a pet?'

'I can't have one,' Sarah said sulkily. 'Nobody'll let me have one. We can't afford it.'

'How about a pet that you wouldn't have to feed and wouldn't have to take to the vet's? Wouldn't cost you anything.'

Sarah looked into his face, trying to understand what he meant. He had, she noticed, blue eyes, but dark hair and dark brows and lashes. She'd never really noticed that about him before. She had always thought that if you had dark hair you had to have dark eyes too. 'I don't know what you mean,' she said. 'You always have to feed pets.'

'Not this kind of pet – ssh! Mother'll come in. I don't want her to know about this – she'd start going on. I'll tell you about it when she's gone to work.' And then Bryan got up and went into the kitchen too.

Sarah looked after him for a moment, wondering what on earth he was talking about. Then she started playing with the kittens again. They were only going to be there for one night, so she had to make the most of them.

Chapter Two

'Do you *have* to take the kittens, Uncle Bryan?'
Sarah said.

Bryan was packing the kittens up in the box again.
He was sitting cross-legged on the kitchen floor with
one little black cat in his hand, stroking it and blowing
gently between its ears. 'I've promised them to people.
Promised 'em weeks ago.'

Sarah, sitting on a chair at the table, nodded sadly.
She knew that she shouldn't have asked but the
kittens had been so funny the night before, chasing
their ping-pong ball. If you made your hand jump
at them, stiff-fingered, they made their legs stiff and
bounced at your hand, wrapped their soft little warm
legs round it, and nipped at your wrist with their hot,
damp little mouths. Their mouths opened in such a
neat little red shape when they mewed. They were
lovely and it hurt to see them go.

She watched the black kitten go into the box,
and wished that she could ask her uncle to get
her one. She wished that Bryan had never brought
the kittens to the house. It would have been
better not to have seen them and not to have
played with them, than to have to give them
up now. 'You said you'd get me a pet,' she

said. 'One that wouldn't need feeding or taking to the vet's.'

All the kittens were in the box and Bryan folded the cardboard flaps down. 'I did, didn't I?' he said, in a way that meant he wished he hadn't.

'You were just teasing, weren't you?' she said. 'There's no such thing as a pet you don't have to feed.'

'There is. No feeding and no vet's bills; and it wouldn't take up space, it wouldn't make any noise or any mess, and it wouldn't shed hair, chew shoes or scratch furniture. The perfect pet.'

Sarah looked at him suspiciously. 'You mean a pet rock,' she said.

'No, I mean a real pet. I'm serious, bab; I'm not teasing. It'd never die either; it'd be with you all your life. But you'd have to keep it a secret and not tell your gran or your mum.'

That made Sarah even more suspicious. 'Why not?'

'Because I'd get into trouble for making it.'

'*Making* it?'

'Ar, making it.'

'I don't want a toy,' Sarah said. 'I've got toys.'

'I know you have and I'm not talking about a toy. I'm talking about an animal – one that moves and's alive. One you can give orders to and it does what you tell it.'

'A robot?' Sarah said.

'A robot! How would I make a robot? It's as much as I can do to put on a plug.'

28

'You can't make an animal,' Sarah said.

'Can't you? Bet you I can.'

Sarah examined his face carefully. He didn't have the expression that was always there, carefully hidden, when he was teasing. He seemed to be telling the truth but she couldn't believe it. 'You can't!' she said, and laughed.

Bryan lost patience. 'All right, I can't. Forget it.' He stood up and lifted the box of kittens. Squealing noises came from inside. 'Behave yourself until your gran comes back,' he said. 'You know all the things that you shouldn't do – don't do any of 'em. And if you need anything, go next door. . . . But your gran shouldn't be too long.'

Sarah opened the door for him and watched him go down the entry to the street. Then she shut the door. The house was instantly very quiet and lonely.

But it was nice to be alone in a house that wasn't hers. She sprawled on the settee for a while with her shoes on the covers, then got up, opened all the drawers and poked through them. She went upstairs and into Bryan's bedroom, which was small and full of sharp, musty green smells from the dried leaves and flowers that hung from his pelmet and filled jars on his chest of drawers. Then she got bored and decided to go up the bank.

She went down the brick path of the ugly garden, ducked low under the branches of the hawthorn tree and scrambled up the bank. She was thinking that she might play at being an Indian hunting monkeys in the rain forest, when she heard voices. She didn't have the bank to herself, as she'd assumed she would have. She saw a flash of bright pink and, going closer through the bushes, saw two other girls.

She immediately felt angry, even cheated. She didn't want other people, strangers, playing on *her* bank. She wanted it all to herself. She didn't like the look of these two anyway. One girl, the older one, had a round chubby face and long blonde hair, held back with a large butterfly grip. She was the one wearing the bright pink dress. The other, a little younger, had brown short hair and wore a green dress. They were very quiet and absorbed about something. They kept moving about a hawthorn tree. Both of them had jam-jars and pieces of card in their hands. She couldn't guess what they were doing.

Then the girl with the blonde hair and the pink dress turned and saw Sarah. She stared at her for a moment, then nudged the girl in the green dress and said, 'Somebody's watching us!' on a sort of rising, singing note. Then giggled. The girl in green stared at Sarah too. 'What do you want?' she said.

'Nothing,' Sarah said, just as aggressively. 'What are you doing?'

'Catching flies,' said the girl in pink.

'Why?' Sarah asked. Instead of answering her they looked at each other and giggled.

'We caught lots in our yard,' the girl in pink said. 'Big, fat bluebottles and greenbottles. They come and land on the bricks in the sun. But we got fed up of that. It's too easy.'

'We thought we'd come and catch some of

these little flies in the trees here,' said the girl in green.

'But you can't catch 'em. They're too small and the leaves get in the way.'

'Why do you want to catch them?' Sarah asked again, but they just laughed. 'My name's Sarah White. I live down there.' She pointed towards her gran's house. I live there so I've more right to be here than you have, was what she meant.

'No you don't,' said the girl in green immediately. 'Mrs Gornal lives there.'

'She's my gran. I'm staying there.'

'We live next door to your gran,' the other girl, the one in pink, said.

'Where Mr and Mrs Griffiths used to live?'

'I don't know who used to live there,' said the girl in pink. 'We moved in last year. My name's Yvette Cornwall and this is my sister Jasmin. Do you want to come and see us catch flies?'

'All right,' Sarah said, and followed them down the steep bank into their back yard. It was just as ugly as her gran's yard but in a different way. Her gran's yard had an old-fashioned ugliness: the Cornwalls' entire garden had been covered with concrete slabs. It was flat and dusty. Some concrete pots had been stood about with plants growing in them, but the pots were so harsh, and the plants looked so imprisoned and puny against their background of concrete, that it made Sarah feel quite hopeless to look at them.

Yvette and Jasmin showed her how easy it was to wait until a fly landed on the edge of a concrete

31

bowl, and then put a jam-jar over it. The fly flew into the upper part of the jar, and they then slipped the piece of card over the jar's mouth and trapped it. They could catch several flies, one after another, in the same jar.

'We've got enough now,' Yvette said. 'Open the shed door.'

Sarah went over and opened the door of the shed. The two other girls followed her. Sarah was surprised to see that the shed wasn't heaped full of tools and rubbish, like every other shed she had ever seen. There was space in this one. There were little gingham curtains over the window, and a counter covered with sticky-backed plastic, and two stools. There were magic-painting books and jars of coloured water on the counter. It had obviously been cleared for the girls to play in.

There was another jar on the counter, with a screwtop lid. Yvette, still keeping her flies trapped inside her jar, stooped to look into this closed jar. 'Look, there's our pet in there,' she said to Sarah with a smile.

Sarah looked closer and saw, at the bottom of the jar, a large grey spider. She could see its little black dots of eyes and its jaws. 'Take the top off,' Yvette said. 'Are you scared to?'

Sarah could see that both the girls were hoping she was scared. She unscrewed the top from the jar. The spider shifted a little on the jar-bottom as the jar wobbled. Yvette put her jar, upside down, on top of the opened jar. Then she pulled the cardboard from between them.

The flies didn't want to go down where the spider was. They kept buzzing back up into the top of the jar Yvette held. She tapped the jar to make them go down. 'Get ready to put the top back on, quick,' she said. 'Now!'

Most of the flies were in the lower jar. Yvette snatched away her jar, and Sarah quickly slammed the screwtop into place and screwed it tight. A couple of the flies escaped, but three of them buzzed about, trapped, in the jar on the counter. Jasmin abandoned her flies, and all three girls bent over the jar to see what would happen.

One of the flies foolishly landed near the spider, and the spider instantly took it. It sat contentedly in the middle of the jar and munched the fly until only the transparent wings were left. These it dropped on the floor of the jar. It made Sarah feel peculiar – cold and creepy. It wasn't the spider that bothered her but the way it chewed, in a rather bored way, on the fly. She'd seen lions eating antelopes on the television, but that was television – not real, somehow. This was real. The fly was alive and buzzing and now it was just a spider-snack, and she was watching from the other side of the glass, not from the other side of a television screen. It made her think of herself, chewing up lambs and pigs and chickens in just that bored way.

'Let's catch some more,' Yvette said. 'We haven't got a jar for you,' she said to Sarah, 'but you can watch.'

But catching flies was boring once you'd mastered it, even with someone to show off to. Yvette soon gave it up and, sitting on the edge of one of the concrete bowls, said to Sarah, 'You say Mrs Gornal's your gran. Where's your mum and dad, then?'

'At home. I'm just staying with my gran. She likes to have me to stay.'

'Mr Gornal's Mrs Gornal's son, isn't he?'

Sarah wondered who 'Mr Gornal' was for a moment. She wasn't used to hearing Bryan called that. She nodded.

'So he's your uncle,' Yvette said, after considering. Then, with a sharp curiosity, she asked, 'What does he do?' Jasmin had stopped catching flies too, and was sitting on a concrete step nearby, listening. 'Is he unemployed?'

She made unemployed sound very bad. Sarah wasn't sure whether Bryan was unemployed or not. He didn't work in a factory or a shop or a school, or anything like that, but did that mean he was unemployed? He went out of the house every day as if he had work to go to, and he had money.

'He doesn't get up until late, does he?' Yvette asked. Jasmin was listening closely and smiling. Not in a friendly way. They were both delighted that Bryan didn't get up until late, because they thought it a disgraceful thing and they were pleased to be able to say so.

'Sometimes he gets up very early,' Sarah said. 'And sometimes he stays out late. That's why he sleeps late.'

'He's on the dole, isn't he?' Yvette said.

Sarah had heard the dole spoken of, but she wasn't completely sure what it was. But they wanted her to agree so that they could sneer. 'No,' she said.

'What does he do for a living then?'

'He works with animals,' Sarah said.

'Doing what?'

'He makes animals better when they're ill,' Sarah said.

'He's a *vet*?' Despite herself, Yvette was impressed.

'Sort of,' Sarah said. 'He does make animals better when they're ill.'

Yvette held out her jam-jar. 'Do you want to have a go at catching flies?'

Sarah was hesitating, not really wanting to but not wanting to refuse, when they all heard the sounds of footsteps coming from the entry between the houses. The sound of a key being put into a lock followed. 'That'll be my gran,' Sarah said, thankfully. 'Got to go now.' She ran up the Cornwalls' concrete garden, scrambled up the bank and through the trees and bushes, and slid down into her grandmother's overgrown and untidy backyard. She ignored Yvette and Jasmin, standing side by side in their yard, watching her run down the path to the kitchen door.

Her gran was already in the kitchen, filling the kettle at the tap. There was another woman sitting at the table, a woman Sarah had never seen before – an oldish woman in a dull brown coat and a soft brown hat. 'That's me granddaughter, Sarah,' Gran Gornal said. 'This is Dot, Sarah. Dot's got a bad back.'

Sarah was feeling shy because Dot was there, and leaned against the wall near the door with her hands behind her. She didn't see what Dot's bad back had got to do with anything.

Once the kettle was on Gran Gornal seated herself opposite Dot at the table, 'Give us that vest, then,' she said.

Dot opened the large handbag she was holding on her lap and took out of it a vest, which she passed across the table to Gran Gornal. Gran Gornal shook it out, held it up, then laid it across her lap and began to stroke it. She sat there, waiting for the kettle to boil, humming the theme tune of a quiz show and stroking the vest. Very odd, Sarah thought.

When the kettle boiled, Dot got up, despite her bad back, and made the tea, while Gran Gornal went on stroking Dot's vest. 'Make our Sarah a sandwich while you're on, Dot, will you? There's cheese in the pantry.'

Dot made them all cheese sandwiches, and Sarah had to come to the table and eat her sandwiches and drink a cup of weak tea. Dot ate and drank and stared through the window at the hawthorn bushes at the top of the garden. Gran Gornal hummed and stroked the vest. Sometimes, when her one hand was occupied with a teacup or a sandwich, she rubbed the vest between the fingers of the other hand. It was very peaceful.

After what seemed to Sarah a very long time, Gran Gornal suddenly handed the vest back across the table to Dot, who put it into her handbag. The two women then got up and gathered their things to go back to work.

'Wash them few cups and things up for me,' Gran Gornal said. 'And *behave*. I shall be back about six. I should hope Bryan'll be back afore then.'

Bryan came home at about four. The first thing he did was to put the kettle on to make himself some tea. Sarah followed him into the kitchen from the front room, where she had been reading about blood-baths in the 'True Detective'.

'Uncle Bryan?' she said. 'Gran came home with a lady today, and she sat and stroked a vest. She just sat, all the time she was here, stroking this vest.'

'What was wrong with her?' Bryan asked.

There was nothing wrong with her. She just stroked this vest.'

'I mean what was wrong with the other woman?' Bryan said. 'It's a cure. It's a way of healing.'

'Oh,' Sarah said. 'She did say that the lady had a bad back.'

'That'd be it then. Her'd wear the vest and it'd make her bad back better, see?'

'Oh,' Sarah said. 'Uncle Bryan?'

'What-an?'

'You said you'd make me an animal?'

'Did I? I never did.'

'Don't tease, Uncle Bryan. You said you would, you know you did. What kind would it be?'

Bryan sat down in a chair by the table. 'If I got you this animal you'd have to be very careful.'

'Oh, I'd look after it really well, Uncle Bryan.'

'I don't mean that,' he said. 'It wouldn't need much looking after. I mean, you wouldn't have to let anybody see it. It's a – very rare sort of animal. You wouldn't have to let your gran see it, or your mum and dad, or *anybody*.'

Sarah didn't like the sound of that. 'What kind of animal is it, Uncle Bryan?' she asked. 'Is it dangerous?'

'It's not dangerous, no. But it might be dangerous to let people know about it.'

'Why?' Sarah asked.

'It just would be!' he said with annoyance, so she didn't ask any more.

'Well, what kind of animal is it? Where would you get it?'

He sat still and seemed to think about this – until the kettle boiled, when he got up suddenly to make the tea. 'Forget it,' he said. 'Forget it, forget it. Bad idea. Sorry I ever said anything about it. Shouldn't be done in this day and age.'

'What?' Sarah said.

'It was all right in Old Devil Gornal's time but not now. Can't do that kind of thing these days. Too risky.'

'Do what?' Sarah shouted.

He put the kettle on the table and then stretched up his arms and cupped his hands behind his head. 'Do what Old Devil Gornal did,' he said. 'Take an old bone and some skin or hair – and make an animal.'

Chapter Three

'How can you *make* an animal?' Sarah said.

'Old Devil Gornal did,' Bryan said.

Sarah felt uneasy. 'That's just a story,' she said. She wanted it not to be true.

Bryan looked away from her, out of the kitchen window to the thick, green hawthorn bushes overhanging the end of the garden. 'No, it's not just a story.'

'How do you know it's not?' Sarah demanded.

'People say it's just a story that we know what's going to happen before it does, but it's not. I knew you were coming on an earlier train, and I got down there to meet you. That wasn't just a story, was it?'

'That's not the same,' Sarah said. 'It's one thing to guess something right like that.' Bryan pulled an impatient face, sat down and hunched himself over the table at the suggestion that he had merely guessed. 'It's another thing to *make* an animal. That's just a story. You're teasing, aren't you? All this about getting me a pet was just a big tease.'

Bryan's tongue poked a lump in his cheek. 'I've made 'em before,' he said. 'Little 'uns. Get a few feathers off a dead bird, and a little knuckle bone out of mother's stew, and you can make a funny little thing. I just did it to see if I could, because I'd heard about Devil Gornal making 'em. Mum used to tell me about how he did, and I went round asking all the old 'uns, all the old Gornals. They all had a bit to tell me. So I tried it out. But only little things, and I took 'em apart again when I was tired of 'em. I was careful never to let 'em get away.'

'You're just teasing again,' Sarah said. 'And anyway, if that's true it was cruel to pull 'em to bits.'

'They're not really alive,' Bryan said. 'Not like a *real* animal . . .' He looked at her disapproving face and ducked his head. 'Well, I suppose it might have been a bit cruel. I didn't think of it like that. I was just tired of 'em and I couldn't let 'em loose, could I? I don't know what they might do.'

'They *are* dangerous, then?' Sarah asked, her heart quickening its beat a little.

'No! No, not so long as somebody's telling them what to do. You see, at first you have to think about 'em, to make 'em do what you want 'em to do – like giving 'em orders. But after a bit they sort of get worked into your mind, and they'll do things even when you aren't thinking about 'em. Well, you *are* thinking about 'em but you don't know you are.'

'I don't know what you mean,' Sarah said.

'Well, it's like – if you're in a good mood with somebody you go on being in a good mood with 'em even when you're busy doing something else and you're not thinking about 'em, don't you? And if you're in a bad mood with 'em, you go on being in a bad mood. It's a different sort of thinking that goes on, sort of *underneath* your ordinary thinking. And, it's that underneath thinking that these things work on. After a while, you don't have to give 'em orders – they're sort of tuned in to you. They're only doing what you want 'em to do, but you might not know what it is that you want 'em to do. . . . So I don't know what might happen if you just let one go. I suppose it might just – just stop, like a broken watch, after a while. It'd be just some feathers and an old bone. But it might go on and on, and I wouldn't know what it was doing because I don't know what I'm thinking half the time. You've got to be really good and really know your own mind, like Old Devil Gornal, before you can keep control of a thing like that. And I didn't want to risk it, so I pulled 'em to bits.'

'I don't believe you,' Sarah said. 'You're making it up.'

'Don't believe me. Forget all about it. I was having you on.'

That made Sarah certain that he was telling the truth. 'Why did Devil Gornal make these things?' she asked. 'Was it for a pet?'

'A pet – Devil Gornal? No. They didn't have pets in them days. Cats was for killing mice, and dogs was for fighting and killing rats. Didn't keep anything unless it was useful.'

'Well, what were these things for then?'

'Bone-dogs,' Bryan said. 'They're called bone-dogs.'

'Well, what was the bone-dog for?' Sarah asked. 'Was it for killing people?'

Bryan glanced across at her. 'No! You always think the worst, don't you? It was a kind of servant. Old Devil sent it out to fetch things and to take messages – to spy for him and to steal for him. Things like that. Anything he wanted it to do, really.'

Sarah sat beside him at the table and leaned across the cloth. She could feel gritty breadcrumbs and sugar crystals pressing into her forearms. 'How would you make it, Uncle Bryan?' She was still watching his face for the signs that would show he was teasing, but she didn't see any sign of them.

'I'd need a bone, a biggish bone – could get one from somebody's Sunday dinner easy enough. I'd need some hair from you, if it's going to be yours, and a spot of blood—'

'Blood!' Sarah said.

'Only a drop, only as much as you'd get by sticking a needle in your finger.'

'I don't want to stick a needle in my finger,' Sarah said.

'You big babby!'

'Stick the needle in *your* finger!'

'It'd be *mine* then,' Bryan said. 'It'd do as I told it. I thought you wanted a pet.'

'Well . . .' Sarah said sulkily. She had, a while ago, stuck a needle in her finger and made it bleed just to see if she was brave enough to do it. Having proved that she was she wasn't very keen to do it again, but she supposed that it might be worth it for a bone-dog.

'Do you want one, then?' Bryan asked.

She looked hard into his face and addressed him formally, hoping to get a serious answer. 'Uncle Bryan, can you really make a bone-dog?'

He nodded. 'Ar.'

'Really, really, really? Honestly and truly?'

He grinned. 'Really, really, really, honestly and truly, I can.'

'Bet you can't,' Sarah said, and watched him even harder.

'I can.' There wasn't a trace of teasing in his voice or face. He was absolutely serious.

Sarah drew a deep breath. 'Well, go on then. I'd like one.'

He looked away from her, stared at the wall. His fingers tapped on the table. 'I don't know whether I should, really. . . . Mother wouldn't like it.'

'You're not much of a witch, are you? Scared of your mum!'

'My mum's a witch too! And a better witch than me,' he said. 'If I do it, you're not to tell your gran, or your mum or your dad, or anybody – promise?'

'I promise. Cross me heart and hope not to die.'

'Especially not your dad. And none of your friends or anybody.'

'I promise,' Sarah said.

'I dunno whether I can trust you.'

'I promise! I won't tell a soul.'

'All right then . . . and I know what we can use. Come on.'

Getting up, he left the kitchen and went through

43

the front room. Sarah hurried after. She scrambled after him up the stairs, which were so steep that she had to go up on all fours. Bryan passed the door of his own bedroom and went into the one Sarah was sharing with her grandmother. All the furniture was old, large and dark. Bryan walked across the creaking floor, unlocked the door of the big wardrobe, and opened it. A smell came out, of old clothes and mothballs. With a clashing of coat-hangers Bryan sorted through coats and dresses, and then produced something from the back of the cupboard and waved it in front of Sarah. 'There you are!'

Sarah put out her hand and held the thing to stop it moving, so she could get a look at it. She almost snatched her hand away at the furry feel of it. It was a fox. There was a tiny fox's head, much smaller than she had ever thought a fox's head would be. Orangey-brown glass eyes stared at her. Tiny white teeth shone from between black lips. Helpless little paws dangled. Bryan was holding it by its long, thick tail.

'What is it?' Sarah asked.

'It's a fox-fur! Women used to wear 'em, like this.' He put it round his own neck, and fastened it so that the fox seemed to be biting its own tail. 'It's a real fox. Dead and tanned. Somebody give it to our mother. Her'd give it you if you asked her for it. Then we could make a bone-dog out of it.'

They grinned at each other, Sarah looking up and Bryan down.

When Gran Gornal came home Sarah was wearing

the fox-fur. Gran Gornal stared at it as she took off her coat. 'Where did you get that?' she asked.

'Bryan gave it me to play with.'

'Some folk make free with other folk's belongings,' Gran Gornal said.

Bryan, from his chair in front of the television, said, 'I didn't think you wanted it.'

'I don't – I never liked it – but it's nice to be asked.'

Sarah stood in front of her grandmother. 'Please, Gran, can I have it, please? I like it!'

'If you want it, have it,' Gran Gornal said roughly. 'No use to me – I think it's a nasty thing. I'd have given it you years ago if I'd have thought you'd want it.'

'Thank you, Gran,' Sarah said. Gran Gornal went through into the kitchen. Sarah scuttled over to Bryan's chair and knelt beside it, giggling.

'I'll get the bone tomorrow,' he said.

Chapter Four

Bryan had gone out somewhere and her gran was at work. Normally Sarah would have enjoyed the novelty of being alone in a different house, able to do all sorts of things without anyone knowing. But that morning things seemed flat and lonely. She sat on the step of the kitchen door, looking at the ugly garden. The wobbly grey and rusty-brown fences were so dispiriting that when she looked at them she felt as if her heart were tugging loose from its usual place as it sank towards her feet. Next door's yard, with its expanse of grubby, featureless concrete, was even worse. Only the hawthorn bushes hanging over the garden from the bank gave her eyes any relief.

Yvette and Jasmin came and looked over the fence at her from their yard. Jasmin wore a red skirt and blue T-shirt today; Yvette had pink dungarees and a white shirt, and looked even more pink and plump and smug than Sarah remembered. But since she was bored and lonely, she was quite pleased to see them. 'Hello,' she said hopefully.

'Your uncle's not a vet!' Yvette said.

'I never said he was a vet.'

'You did!' Jasmin said.

'He's not a vet, he's just unemployed,' Yvette said.

'I asked my mum. She says you have to go to college and everything to be a vet. You have to have letters after your name. Your uncle's never been to college. He draws the dole.'

Sarah got up from the step and went towards them, still hoping to explain. 'He's not a *vet*, but he heals animals. People ask him to heal their animals.'

'How does he heal them if he's not a vet?' Yvette asked.

Sarah thought of her gran stroking a vest to make Dot's bad back better. And, in other years, she had seen Bryan gently stroking and stroking the animals he'd been asked to cure – even a big, red-kneed spider. He'd stroked it with one finger and had tried to get her to stroke it too, but she wouldn't. She hadn't understood then that stroking was the way he cured. 'He strokes them,' she said.

'Strokes them? You don't make things better by stroking them!'

'My uncle does! And my gran!'

'Liar. You're making it up to show off,' Yvette said.

Jasmin said, 'You're stupid.'

'No, you're stupid,' Sarah said, 'because you don't know what you're on about.'

'Oh, listen to who's talking! Listen to who's calling us stupid!' Yvette said. 'Somebody who thinks you can make things better by stroking them!'

'She's a loony,' Jasmin said, and Yvette looked at her sister and smiled.

'Yeah, a loony,' she agreed.

'You just don't know,' Sarah said. 'My gran's got second sight and so has my uncle. They know about things that haven't happened yet. And they can heal—'

'Loony!' Yvette said, and Jasmin sniggered.

'I'm not a loony! *Listen!*'

'Loony!' Jasmin said, before Sarah could go on.

'Listen a minute—' Sarah wanted to tell them how Bryan had known that she'd be coming on an earlier train even though no one had told him. She wanted to tell about her gran knowing where the missing ring was, and knowing that a bomb would fall on the street.

'Loony, loony, loony!' Yvette said in a sing-song chant.

'Loony, loony, loony!' Jasmin chorused. Both of them kept chanting and laughing and pointing. Their laughter wasn't altogether natural. They wanted to make Sarah feel like a complete joke, so they forced it a bit. They also wanted to make it impossible to hear anything she had to say. Every time Sarah tried to explain, they chanted more loudly, and shrieked with false laughter, and jabbed at her with their fingers. It was infuriating. She felt her face getting very red and tears coming to her eyes. She didn't want to cry in front of them. She turned her back on them and walked very briskly across the yard and into the kitchen, shutting the door behind her.

Yvette and Jasmin burst into real, natural laughter, and shouted, 'Scared-baby, scared-baby!'

'Sarah's run away, Sarah's run away!'

'Sarah's a loony, Sarah's a loony!'

Sarah went through into the front room. She could still hear them there, though very faintly, chanting, 'Loony, loony, loony!' She lay down on the settee, her face on its dusty covers. 'Sticks and stones may break your bones, but words can never hurt you,' her mother always said, and Sarah had always thought it was a stupid thing to say because it was so plainly not true. Words did hurt, very much. She kept still, hoping that the quiet hum of the room would soothe the sore, scratchy pain of the name-calling, but it couldn't. So she cried, and lifted up her voice and bawled, and made a wet place on the settee; and after she'd grown bored with crying she did feel better. She sat up and began to think of all the things she'd like to do to Yvette and Jasmin. Punch their ugly faces. Pull their hair. Make them break out in spots. Break their legs. Scratch them, kick them. She wished them belly-aches and headaches and all things painful and bad. Back-aches, toothaches, the worst growing-pains ever.

She suddenly remembered her gran stroking the vest for Dot to wear, so her bad back would be better. Slowly the thought pieced itself together in her mind: if her gran could make Dot's bad back better by stroking a vest, then wouldn't she be able to make Dot's bad back worse by doing much the same thing? By punching the vest, maybe.

She thought further. Bryan could make animals better by stroking them. Then wouldn't he be able to make an animal ill by stroking it, if he wanted to? After all, if you can switch a thing on you can switch it off. If you can make something you can also smash it.

The sad thing about wishing headaches and broken legs on people who've hurt you is that, usually, you can only wish it. It makes you feel better for a while, but it also makes you feel foolish, because no matter how bad the things you wish on them, nothing happens to them. They hurt you, and laugh, and get away with it to come back and laugh at you another day.

If only she'd been born a true Gornal, like her gran and Bryan. Then she'd be able to make them sorry. She'd make them think twice about who was stupid. Far from getting away with it, and laughing at her again, they'd cringe when they saw her coming. They'd try to butter her up, and offer her sweets, and do everything they could to get on her right side. But she would never forget what they'd done. Instead of taking their favours she'd just give them another headache, another toothache. And serve them right.

Bryan could do it. It was no good asking her gran. She'd just say, 'Fight your own battles.' But Bryan would if she asked him. Bryan was generous, even her father said so. He'd do almost anything for you if you asked him.

Bryan came home at about twelve, bringing two meat pies with him. He crouched in front of the oven to light it. Sarah, standing beside him, said, 'I don't like those girls next door.'

'Don't you?'

'They call me names. They call me "loony".' Bryan laughed. 'It's not funny,' Sarah said sternly.

He'd lit the oven, and he stood up and began to fill the kettle. 'No, bab, it ain't. But what d'you expect me to do about it?'

The perfect opportunity. Sarah stood tall, took a deep breath, and said, 'I want you to make 'em ill. Teach 'em a lesson.'

'You want me to what?'

'Make 'em ill. I want you to give 'em sore throats and belly-ache and headache. You could do that, couldn't you?'

Bryan lit the gas under the kettle. 'I suppose I could if I tried hard enough. But I ain't going to.'

'Oh, why not?'

Bryan went over to the table and sat on one of the chairs. 'Because it'd be a fool's game.'

'They deserve it,' Sarah said. 'They deserve worse – they say you can't heal, you know. They say you're unemployed and a loony!'

She was disappointed when Bryan only laughed again, and put his hands behind his head. She'd expected him to be angry.

'You could do something about it!' she said.

'Oh, look bab. . . . Have you ever seen "Frankenstein"?'

Sarah was sulky and wary. She couldn't see what 'Frankenstein' had got to do with it. 'No. I'm not allowed to see horror films.'

'Well, Frankenstein's a scientist who makes a monster out of dead bodies. He cuts up lots of bodies and sews 'em together into one big one. Then he hauls it up through the roof in the middle of a thunder and lightning storm, and brings it to life. And it goes on the rampage, running through the countryside and killing people. And *then* it comes back and kills Frankenstein, who made it. See?'

'No,' Sarah said.

'He made the monster, and then the monster kills him. Because he might have made it, but he can't control it once he's made it.'

'Well, what's that got to do with anything?' Sarah said.

Bryan sighed. 'Don't you remember what I was telling you about the bone-dogs? Don't you listen to anything? After a while they get a sort of life of their own, you remember? It's a bit like that when you start wishing things on people. After a while the wish gets a life of its own. It goes on working whether you're wishing for it to or not.'

'Well?' Sarah said.

'Well, Miss, if you've wished something good on somebody then it don't matter much if it does go on working by itself, doesn't it? But wishing bad on people can be a very dangerous thing to do – for the person who does the wishing, I mean. The bad wish can come back on you.'

'Oh, you're just saying that,' Sarah said.

'No, it's true. You don't know what you're thinking yourself half the time. Nobody does. Suppose you wish a terrible headache on somebody and suppose you feel just a little bit guilty about it. Suppose, just for a fraction of a second, so quickly that you don't notice it yourself, you think, "I'm so bad for wishing a headache on her that I ought to have one twice as bad . . ." You see?'

'Oh . . .' Sarah said. 'You mean – then you'd get a headache twice as bad.'

'That's right,' Bryan said. 'Now, I don't wish anything bad on the two little girls next door anyway, whatever they say about me. They'm just babbies. But even if I did I wouldn't do anything about it, because I'd be sure to feel guilty about it later, and then kybosh! I'd be suffering from me own bad wish. Like Frankenstein being limbed by his own monster. You have to be careful about these things.'

'I wouldn't mind a bit of a headache, if they had bad ones as well,' Sarah said. 'If I could wish things on 'em, I still would.'

'More fool you, then,' Bryan said.

Sarah sat at the table and watched him bring the filled teapot to it, and fetch cups from the cupboard. She watched him open the oven and touch the top of the pies to see if they were done enough. 'It's not fair,' she said. 'It's not asking much. I bet you're not going to make that animal you promised to make me either. You never keep your promises, you.'

'Niggle, niggle, niggle,' Bryan said, putting a plate with a meat pie on it in front of her. 'For your information, Madam, there's a plastic bag in the other room with a bone in it. I got it from a friend of mine this morning.' He cut open his pie and let the steam out. 'We could make it tonight,' he said. 'After your gran's gone to bed. At midnight.' In a ghostly voice he added, 'The witching hour.'

'Well,' Gran Gornal said that night. 'I'm for bed. Come on, Sarah.'

'Oh, Gran,' Sarah said, 'I want to stay up.'

'Ain't you stayed up long enough? It's getting on for twelve o'clock.'

' "Dracula's Risen From the Grave" 's on,' Bryan said. 'Her wants to see it.'

Gran Gornal stopped on her way to the stairs and looked at them suspiciously. ' "Drakoola's Risen From His Grave"? Ain't that an horror film?'

Bryan made a contemptuous noise. 'They have worse things on the school programmes these days, Mother. It's just a laugh.'

'Please, Gran, let me see it,' Sarah said.

'We'm going to have a giggle at the tomato ketchup,' Bryan said.

'I'll bet your mother and father wouldn't let you see a film like that,' Gran Gornal said. 'Especially your father.'

'Oh, don't be a pain, Mother,' Bryan said. 'It's nothing, I tell you. . . . Look, if it's frightening her I'll switch it off and send her to bed. I promise.'

'I wonder you ain't off out tonight,' his mother said, scowling at him.

'Gets boring, going out night after night,' Bryan said. 'Felt like staying in and watching the box. That's all right with you, ain't it? Go on, get off to bed.'

Sarah wondered if she'd ever dare to talk to her parents like that. And Gran Gornal went. Slowly, and with suspicious backward looks, but she went. With grins on their faces they listened to her footsteps thumping up the stairs, and the ceiling creaking as she crossed the room upstairs. But when Sarah's thoughts suddenly switched to what they were really staying up for, her grin vanished.

Bryan pulled a plastic carrier bag out from between his chair and the wall, and began to check over its contents. Sarah sat on the floor beside him. The bag held the fox-fur, which Sarah took out of Bryan's hands. She liked looking at it. The glass eyes were almost real, the light shone through such depths in them. She liked touching the dry little pads on the limply hanging paws, and stroking the dry, dusty fur. 'Poor little thing,' she said. 'I thought foxes were bigger than this. Poor, poor little thing.'

The fur looked a little odd now because while Gran Gornal had still been at work Bryan had taken a big, curved cobbler's needle and some thick twine, and had sewn up the edges of the fur so that it made an odd sausage shape, with paws hanging crookedly. There was a small hole left under the jaws.

'Here,' said Bryan. From the plastic bag he'd taken a long, thin bone. It was white and dry, yellowish in places and pale, greyish-blue in others. Sarah held the fox-fur, and he poked the bone through the hole under the jaw and down inside the sewn-up skin. Next, from the bag, he took a pair of scissors and a small ball of plasticine. He put the scissors on the arm of his chair, and began squeezing the plasticine in his hands to soften it. When it was soft he took the scissors and snipped a piece from Sarah's hair, from underneath where it wouldn't show. Then he squeezed the hair and the plasticine together until they were thoroughly mixed. 'Cut your nails,' he said, nodding at the scissors.

Sarah snipped pieces from her nails and stuck them into the ball of plasticine. Bryan dropped the ball of hair, plasticine and nails inside the fox-fur, with the bone. Then he looked at his watch and said, 'Come on; we'll get the lantern.'

What Bryan called a lantern was a large, battery-operated electrical light that stood upright and had a handle to carry it by. It was kept at the back of the pantry, and he sent Sarah in to search for it because the roof of the pantry sloped down almost to the floor. Even Sarah had to stoop, and she had to poke about among mops and packs of firelighters, bundles of plastic bags, wellington boots, cans of polish and bundles of candles. There was a strong scent of old greenery from the dried herbs hanging in there. She found the light eventually and brought it out, but she said, 'Shouldn't we be using candles?'

'Why?'

'Well . . . it's more witchy.'

'It's more blow-outy as well. Candles! Look, a light's a light. Now come on.'

Sarah followed him out into the yard. It was a shock to step down from the doorstep. Suddenly they were outside, and it was night. The air was cool and damp although it was August, and it came and touched their faces as if it were alive. The night and the dampness had soothed all the sounds of the town. Cars crooned along the road, the wind sighed heavily in the hawthorn bushes. They walked down the garden path, sensing the slippery moss under their feet and feeling the long grass rasp at their hands and clothes. A smell of dampness and greenery and *living* rose to them as their feet crushed leaves. Sarah shivered, but not with cold. She didn't think she'd noticed before how utterly different night was from day.

The branches and leaves of the hawthorns rustled as Bryan moved them aside. He stepped up the bank easily and reached down a hand to help Sarah. He gave a great pull on her arm and lifted her up – for a second it was like a fun-fair ride.

Once they were on the bank and hidden under the hawthorns, Bryan switched the light on. It was so brilliant in the darkness that it blinded them, then they were only dazzled. Sarah, blinking, looked round and saw that the leaves very close to the light were as bright as emeralds, but those only a little way away were grey and black, as if they were part of a black and white photograph. And beyond that, now the light was on, they could see nothing – only darkness. The light lit them a small area, already flickered with the dancing shadows of moths, but it made the rest of the night seem even bigger and colder and wider and impenetrable.

Bryan picked up the light and carried it away in

one hand, the bag crumpled in his other. He went up the bank and Sarah clawed her way after him, slipping on the steep slope because of her hurry. She was nervous of being too far from the light because, though she knew that this little patch of woodland was only a few metres square and surrounded by roads and houses on all sides, it seemed lost and distant from all things friendly in depths of darkness and night. She wanted to keep close by Bryan, who was used to the witching hour.

But Bryan didn't go far. He stopped near the elder and held the light high so that they could see the clusters of creamy white flowers growing in polka-dot patches among the leaves.

'Elder,' Bryan said. 'Hawthorn and elder are our trees.' He set the light down on the ground and it threw light up into the elder tree, giving colour to the lowest leaves and flowers but leaving all the rest grey, like grey lace. Bryan crouched beside it, put the rustling, crackling plastic bag on the ground and took the fox-fur from it. Holding the odd, limp little fox, he looked about at the night as if checking something. 'Waxing moon,' he said. 'Know what that means?'

'No,' Sarah whispered.

'Means the moon's getting bigger, growing towards full moon. You always use the waxing moon for anything you want to grow – or live. Now. The blood.'

Sarah had known this was coming. She held her hand out but said hopefully, 'We haven't brought a needle.'

'I have.' Bryan took a needle from the cloth of the breast pocket on his shirt. The slender metal gleamed in the light of the lamp. 'Shall I do it or do you want to do it yourself?'

Sarah tried to decide whether it was better to jab yourself or have someone else do it, and pulled a face in her indecision.

'Probably be over quicker if I do it,' Bryan said.

'No, I'll do it.' She took the needle from him, reluctant but determined.

Bryan held the fox-fur out, holding open the hole beneath the jaw. 'Drip some blood in there, inside it.'

Sarah motioned at her finger with the needle, so half-heartedly that she didn't even feel the point. She tried again and felt the point enter her skin. It hurt but drew no blood, and she heard Bryan sigh. That made her angry, and she stabbed at her finger so that the needle went in deep and hurt a great deal. A large round globule of blood, glistening black in the poor light, welled up on her fingertip. It ran down, curling round her finger, and then dripped off into the fox-fur.

'That's enough,' Bryan said, and she stuck her finger in her mouth, sucking on the iron taste of blood. She sat on the damp grass and leaves, feeling cold moisture soak into her clothes, and watched as Bryan sewed up the rest of the fox. This is silly, she suddenly thought. It can't work. How can it work? How can a bone and some blood, nails and hair sewn into an old fox-fur possibly come to life? It's just silly. Bryan was working clumsily, having to use a great deal of strength to force the needle through the fox-fur and to pull the thread after it.

'There,' Bryan said under his breath, after he had knotted off the thread and bitten it through. He laid the sewn-up fox-fur on the ground. It lay there, a strange shape, its head, paws and brush twisted at odd angles by the clumsy stitching. It looked very sad and rather like a fox – like a fox that's been knocked down and killed, and is lying at the side of the road.

'I wonder how long poor old Foxy's been dead?' Bryan said, his voice low and whisperingly hoarse in the darkness under the trees. 'It's been a good long time since fox-furs was in fashion. It'll be a laugh to bring him back, won't it?'

'Will it be a fox then?' Sarah whispered, rather throatily. She thought about what it might mean to bring the dead fox back to life. Surely it would be angry with the people who'd killed it? And it might not know that it hadn't been them.

'Dunno what it'll be,' Bryan said. 'It's a fox-fur, a sheep's bone, and your blood, hair and nails. Pretty funny mixture.' He lookd up and Sarah quickly looked up too, to see why. She saw the sky above her, the deepest blue, touched with darker shades. Faintly against it, she saw the shapes of thickly leaved branches – and then, drifting, brilliant, sharply silhouetting dozens of tiny leaves, a thin, white, crescent moon. She felt the touch of the cold wind again, as a new thing. The wind was almost like the voice of the moon.

She heard a sound and looked at the earth again. It was hard to see after the brightness of the moon and against the harsher brightness of the lamp – but then she saw that Bryan was feeling the fox-fur all over. And he had a stone, a big stone, which he gripped in his hand, reminding her suddenly of drawings of cavemen using stone-axes, which they had to grip with their whole hand. He touched the stone to fox-fur and raised it, as if to strike, but didn't. He only mimed the act of striking, measuring the blow. She wanted to ask what he was doing, but as she was about to speak a sort of fright gripped her and stopped her. She was seized with a sudden conviction – a certain knowledge – that the houses and roads were not only cut off from them by darkness, but *no longer there*. She couldn't hear anything from them: no engines, no radios – but she could feel the emptiness echoing back to her. And all around her, in dampness rising from the earth, in dampness drifting down like finest rain from the moon, was something: an earth smell, a muddiness, a liveness. The grasses and leaves around them seemed to lean over their shoulders, touching them like friends – eerie friends – as if the elder and hawthorn wanted to see what they were doing. It was frightening, and yet, in the midst of it all, Bryan, in his crouching, caveman's pose, still wore his shirt from Tesco's and his jeans from off the market. Sarah moved much closer to him and clung to his arm, partly for the sake of that Tesco shirt: surely they could never be lost in the change she felt about them, while that shirt and those jeans, and her own British Home Stores clothes were there, to act as a talisman.

Bryan looked up at the moon again, then brought the stone down on the fox-fur and whispered something. What did you say? Sarah wanted to ask. Is that the magic? Is it only words that are going to make a dry fox-fur a living thing? But she could feel stronger magic all around them: it blazed down on them from the soft brilliance of the moon. It filled that narrow, wild space between the rows of houses and the tarmac'd roads.

Bryan raised the stone again, and again he whispered and smashed the stone down on the fox-fur. And again. And then Bryan pushed himself away from the fox-fur, pushed himself further up the bank, and sat looking at the animal skin expectantly as it lay in the light of the lamp, dappled by moth-shadows.

Sarah stared too – then gasped and moved towards Bryan as the fox-fur moved – but it hadn't moved. It was just a trick of the shadows thrown by the fluttering insects. Of course it hasn't worked, Sarah thought. What did you expect? Bryan would start laughing in a minute, at having caught her out. It was just a big tease. And he'd caught her out properly.

The tricky light made it seem to move again and then Sarah's flesh seemed to take a great leap upwards from her bones with fright as something much bigger moved nearby. It was Bryan. Of course. The electric light, shining upwards instead of down, threw such odd shadows that his slight movement on the edge of her vision had come as a great shock. He leaned towards the fox-fur and held out his hand – and the nose of the fox-fur lifted to touch it.

Sarah held her breath, and her heart pounded on in the vacuum. She stared at her uncle's hand, and the sniffing fox's nose until her eyes ached. It couldn't be. It couldn't be.

Her eyes saw – and her brain denied – that the fox-fur's nose had shifted from Bryan's hand and had swung round to her. She heard her own breath pass her ears in a sudden snatched gasp.

Quietly, Bryan said, 'Give it your hand, Sarah. Gently, though. Don't frighten it.'

Don't frighten *it*? She remembered the little teeth she had seen between the dry, dead lips, and shook her head without knowing she was shaking it. But no, no, no – she couldn't hold out her hand to those dead little teeth.

'Sarah, let it know you – give it your hand.'

She simply shook her head.

Then the fur made a big movement – it heaved itself up, and fell back. Through the soft sound of the breeze she heard harsher, scratchier movements as those dry little paws scrabbled at the ground. It heaved again. It was dragging itself towards her.

She gave a loud cry of disgust and pushed herself backwards, away from it, and half fell, half slithered down the bank. She was scratched, bruised and stung by nettles when she found herself at the bottom. Shocked, a little bewildered, she still managed to pick herself up and hurry along the bottom of the bank, ducking under branches, slapped in the face by leaves and twigs. The way she had to go seemed longer than it had been on the way there, and she began to feel a terror that she had been right, and the houses had all vanished. But then she found the opening under the hawthorn trees that led into her gran's garden, and ran down the path and into the kitchen. There, enclosed by the safe brick walls and the safe, dingy yellow light, she stopped, breathing hard and trembling.

She calmed a little more, pushed her hair out of her eyes and went through into the front room. There the light was brighter, and on the television Dracula was spreading his scarlet-lined cloak to the sound of spooky music. Sarah flopped down into one of the big, soft armchairs and looked about, at the flowered carpet on the floor, the flowered paper on the walls, the used cups on the coffee table. Nothing out of the ordinary could happen in here. It all looked so snug, so smug.

She heard her uncle come in at the kitchen door. He came through into the front room, carrying the lamp, and kicked the door shut in something of a temper. 'A fine one you am!' he said. 'What you run away for? It's easy to see you ain't got much Gornal in you.'

She looked away from him, embarrassed, and having nothing to say. A second later, peeping at him to see what he was going to do now, she saw him taking something gently from inside his jacket – gently as if it were a kitten. She sat up straight when she saw that it was the fox-fur. He held it up in his hand as if it were a kitten, stroked it with one finger and kissed his mouth at it – and she saw the little pointed head with the bright glass eyes swing round towards her.

'Stop it, Uncle Bryan!' she shouted.

'Stop what? What am I doing?'

'Stop making it do that! You're only trying to frighten me. Stop working it!'

'I'm not working it. What's the matter with you? I told you I could make a bone-dog, didn't I? Well, here it is.'

Still sitting upright and stiff, Sarah said, 'I don't believe it – throw it outside.'

Bryan frowned. He was becoming annoyed. 'I won't throw it anywhere. Now you're being cruel, Sarah. Your blood's in it, that's why it wants to come to you. It won't hurt you – it can't. You wouldn't hurt yourself, would you?' Slowly, still holding the nasty little thing, he went to his knees beside Sarah's chair. The fox-fur stretched out its neck, pointing its sharp nose towards her, just like a real animal that's curious and wants to be stroked. 'Stroke it,' Bryan said. 'It won't hurt you. It's not hurting me, is it?'

'But it's—' She couldn't think of one word that would sum up the nastiness of the old, dusty dead skin, the bone and the nail clippings, the blood and glass eyes.

Bryan's frown was angrier. 'It's *alive* now,' he said. 'So be kind to it. You stroked it before.'

'That was when it was only an old fox-fur,' Sarah said, staring at the way the ears flicked and the head stretched towards her.

'It's just an old fox-fur now. Oh, have some guts, wench!'

The idea that she was being cowardly stung her. She stretched out her hand, almost touched the thing's head, and withdrew hastily when the head turned up towards her hand. Then she steadied herself and put two fingers between the pointed ears. The fur was still dusty and it wasn't at all warm, but it wasn't nasty either. When the little head pressed upwards against her hand she gave a nervous, pleased giggle. 'And you're not working it?' she asked Bryan.

'See for yourself,' he said, and put the bone-dog on the arm of her chair.

It wasn't very skilful at getting about on its boneless legs. It tumbled from the chair-arm into the chair beside her. It lifted up its head, its ears pointed, and its warm, orangey-brown glass eyes shining at her. Its thick tail twitched, twitched again, and then managed a couple of swings.

'Look, it's wagging its tail!' Sarah said. She was filled with thrills of fear and laughter mixed: it was wonderful discovering that there was nothing to be afraid of after all. She put her hands under the strange little creature and lifted it on to her lap. It felt rather odd: fragile and lumpy, like a poorly stuffed toy. On her lap it felt very light, and it wasn't warm. It wasn't cold either, but it had none of the warmth you expect from a puppy or kitten. It pushed its front paws against her – though she hardly felt it – and raised up its head to stare at her. Its mouth opened, showing tiny white teeth in a grin. It seemed very glad to be with her.

'What shall I call it?' she said, still stroking it. She felt breathless and giggly.

'Fido?' Bryan said.

'That's a dog's name and it's a fox. Foxy? No, I don't like that. I know "Reynardine".' She said the name impressively, because it was strange-sounding and foreign. 'That's a fox's name, isn't it?'

'I don't know, is it?' Bryan said.

'Like "Reynard",' Sarah said. 'Can I play with him, like with a real pet?'

'You can do whatever you like,' Bryan said. 'It's yours. But don't let your gran see it.'

Chapter Five

It was easy to teach Reynardine tricks. She held out her arm close to the floor, and Reynardine jumped over it. She held bits of paper over its head, and it sat up to beg. She rolled an old, dented ping-pong ball under the chairs, and it flopped and scuttled over the carpet, rather like a seal, to fetch it back. It wagged its tail in a very funny un-foxlike way and grinned, as if it were panting. But it wasn't panting. She didn't think it could breathe.

In a very short time she grew fond of it. It was so funny, the way it stumbled and rolled on its back as it ran after the ping-pong ball, and lay there, wiggling its legs like a beetle until she put it right way up again. And when she threw the ball into a chair it bravely tried to climb into the chair to fetch it, scrabbling and scrabbling away at the front of the chair. It didn't seem able to jump that high and it couldn't get enough grip to climb, but it seemed prepared to go on trying for ever.

Whenever her gran was heard coming home – when she heard her footsteps echoing from the roof of the entry or her voice calling to neighbours, or when she heard her gran's key in the lock – Sarah would hide Reynardine wherever she could. She would stuff it under the settee or armchairs, behind the deep frill that ran around the bottoms of them. Once, when she was in the kitchen, she went into the pantry and hid the fox-fur amongst all the cans and bottles on the floor in there. Another time, caught away from these hiding-places, she hid it under her cardigan until she had a chance to put it somewhere else. She remembered a story she'd heard about a soldier who hid a fox – a real fox – under his cloak, and the fox ate his innards out and killed him. It made her rather nervous. Reynardine did whatever she told it to do. Would merely thinking about that story make Reynardine start gnawing at her? But in fact Reynardine didn't so much as twitch.

The nearest her gran came to catching her was when she was playing in the yard one day and Gran Gornal came in at the gate behind her. Sarah gasped for a moment, but then grabbed Reynardine by the scruff and moved him up and down as if she were making him move, as she might any stuffed toy. She lifted him up to show her gran. 'I sewed him up, look, and made him look like a real fox.'

Her gran didn't look pleased. 'Hmm,' she said. 'Might have known it'd come to its last home with you.' She meant that Sarah had ruined the fox-fur by sewing it up. 'Can't leave nothing be, can you?' And her gran had gone into the kitchen in a bad temper.

Sarah began taking the bone-dog on to the bank among the trees. She was quite happy to go there and to play in the yard, because she hadn't seen anything of Yvette and Jasmin for days. Her gran said she thought they'd gone on holiday. Sarah hoped it was a really long holiday – a six weeks' holiday. Then she'd have gone home before they came back, and she wouldn't ever have to see them again. They might have moved house again before next year.

On the bank she hid a creamy white pebble under the hawthorn tree, and then sent the bone-dog to fetch it. She sat near the opening to her gran's garden and listened to the rustling as the bone-dog half-dragged itself and half-walked through the grass and leaves. It took a long time, so long that she lay down on the bank among the flowers and grass and closed her eyes.

At first she saw what everyone sees when they close their eyes on a sunny day – an oval of red, blurry darkness, barred by shifting shadows. But then a spot of greater darkness seemed to form in the oval, a little off-centre. Then it seemed to open or to expand, but as it expanded it stopped being darkness and became sight, even though she had her eyes closed. It was like looking through a tiny circular window which was quickly growing bigger and bigger, so that she could see more and more. Through this window she saw grass blades, thick and juicy and sharp, as if they were very close. Round grass stems with leaves sheathing from them. Large leaves – a large, scuttling spider, big as her thumb. . . .

She opened her eyes and sat up, more surprised than frightened. Nothing like that had ever happened to her before. It hadn't been like something she'd thought or imagined – it had been like something she had *seen*, without expecting to.

She looked round at the big trees and the small grasses and realized, from the change in size, that she had seen the grasses and the leaves as she might have done if she had been down among them, as if she'd been very small. She lay on her belly and put her face down among the leaves, but it didn't look the same . . . and then, rustling through the grass, struggling back towards her, grinning, with the pebble between its teeth, came Reynardine. It came right up to her, until their noses touched. Then it dropped the pebble and wagged its tail.

She closed her eyes again and this time the darkness behind them was complete, since her face was turned from the sun. And yet again that tiny round window appeared and swelled and widened – and through it, though her eyes were tightly closed, she saw the sky and the trees against it, and a larger, darker, bulkier shape rearing up against them. It moved. It was a head – the almost silhouetted head and shoulders of someone. A big person, she thought at first, but then saw that it was the head of a girl with untidy hair floating about her head in rat's tails . . . it was her!

The shock made her open her eyes quickly, and then she was seeing again – but with sight a little sharper-edged and more brightly coloured than when her eyes were closed. She saw the grass in front of her and, lying crouched in it, almost like a dog, the odd shape of the sewn-up fox-fur. The pebble lay in front of its paws,

She felt sick, rather as she did on fun-fair rides when she was swung violently from one travelling direction into another. She picked up the fox-fur, went inside, and told Bryan about it.

'You're a Gornal after all!' he said.

'But it makes me feel sick – it scares me,' she said. 'It's not right.'

'What d'you mean, it's not right?'

'It's not normal,' she said.

Bryan stooped and looked into her face. 'It's happening, isn't it? And it's not hurting you, is it? So it must be normal. Don't worry about it! Just enjoy it!'

That night she left the bone-dog outside. Late, after it was dark, she ran up the garden path and tossed the fox-fur up through the hawthorn shadows, into the long grass of the bank. Going back towards the house she thought how wonderful it would be to stay out all night, all night long. Watching it get darker and darker – how dark did it get? And what was it like to see the light beginning to come again? How quickly did it come?

She couldn't sleep for a long time. What if someone found Reynardine and took it away? But who would be walking over the bank in the middle of the night? Real foxes might. A real fox might find the bone-dog and rip it to bits. Or, if there weren't any foxes, dogs or cats might.

Her thoughts wandered off into patterns of leaves,

and a constant noise in her ears of leaves touching, leaves rubbing and rustling, and a great sweeping, soughing sigh that came from above, where the taller trees swayed their tops in the breeze. It was very dark and she could only see the faintest grey shapes of things picking their way through the leaves, with a scratch of claws and a drag and a rustle – eyes shone for a second – mice! There were mice! And something much bigger and much quieter, moving with the quietness of fur, unrustling, through the leaves. She lay down deeper in the leaves that covered her as the cat went by.

The time that passed was long and short at the same time. Nothing happened except for the noises and the passings-by among the leaves. A greyer blue crept into the darkness and, looking up, there was a pinkness above the dark layer of leaves that hid the sky, and then a paler, more silvery light, though it was still faint.

And then the light was much brighter, and the noise of the leaves shifting in her ears seemed more like the creaking of bedsprings – and she came awake with a jump in her gran's old bed. It was morning and her gran was already up. The pictures of her dream kept floating through her head, and getting between her and what she could really see. She had to shake her head to clear them away. And when they were quite gone, she only had to close her eyes for another kind of vision to return: the bone-dog was lying in the grass of the bank, looking between the stems at Gran Gornal's ugly back garden and the red brick of the house. And when she closed her eyes Sarah could see what the bone-dog could see. She sat up in bed, feeling a great glow of satisfaction and pleasure. She was a Gornal, after all, despite being half a White. When she grew up she'd be able to heal, like her gran and uncle. She'd be able to tell people's fortunes and save them from death in plane and train crashes.

But when she left the house by the back door to fetch Reynardine from the bank, the first thing she saw was Yvette and Jasmin Cornwall, sitting on a concrete ledge in their back yard.

Chapter Six

As soon as they saw Sarah, Yvette called out, 'Hello!' She seemed quite friendly, as if they'd never quarrelled.

Sarah didn't say anything. She carried on walking towards the bank to fetch Reynardine, but then wondered if she should, with the other girls watching. She stopped, uncertainly, among the long grass and overgrown rhubarb of her gran's garden.

Yvette came to the fence, followed by Jasmin. 'We wondered if you'd still be here,' she said. 'We've been on holiday. We went touring in Scotland.'

'I hope it rained all the time,' Sarah said.

'It did rain, quite a bit, but we didn't mind. We went to see Edinburgh Castle. I've got a kilt – do you want to see it?'

'No,' Sarah said, and went on up the path. She'd get Reynardine and take him back to the house. They'd only think he was a toy, so it didn't matter if they saw him.

Yvette and Jasmin walked up their own yard, keeping level with her. 'Why are you being so nasty?' Yvette asked.

'You were nasty to me,' Sarah said.

'When?' Yvette asked, in genuine surprise.

'Before you went on your holiday.'

'But that was two weeks ago! And we weren't nasty anyway. Were we?' she asked Jasmin.

Jasmin agreed that they hadn't been.

Sarah reached the hawthorns at the end of the garden, ducked into their dusty, gnat-filled shade, and clambered up the bank they grew on. She stood among the leaves and grass, looking round, and saw the dusty greyish-red of Reynardine's fur. She stooped quickly and grabbed him up, straightening just as Yvette and Jasmin became visible, climbing up the bank from their garden.

'You're very touchy,' Yvette said. 'I only pointed out that your uncle wasn't a vet, that's all. Fancy getting all worked up about that!'

Jasmin was staring at Reynardine curiously. 'What's that?' she asked.

'I never said my uncle was a vet. I said he healed animals and he does, and you were very rude about him.' She clutched Reynardine tightly, partially hiding him in her arms.

'What's that?' Jasmin asked again, and came a bit closer.

'It's mine,' Sarah said crushingly.

'Let me see it.'

'No,' Sarah said.

'Now who's being rude?' Yvette cried. 'She only wants to have a look at it – it looks a dirty old thing to me anyway.'

'It's better than anything *you* could have,' Sarah said, and slipped back down the bank into her gran's garden. She was marching down the path towards the kitchen door when she heard noises behind her. Turning, she saw that Yvette and Jasmin had climbed down into her garden too. Unbelieving indignation filled her. How *dared* they?

'Get out of my gran's garden!' she said.

'We're not in your gran's garden,' Jasmin yapped back immediately.

Sarah had no answer to that. What a stupid thing to say, since they were plainly in her gran's garden.

'There's no fence, is there?' Yvette said. 'There's nothing to say that's the bank and this is the garden. It all runs into one – so we're not in your gran's garden. We've got a right to be here.'

'Get out!' Sarah shouted.

'Make us,' said Yvette.

All right, Sarah thought. You've asked for it. I will. She put Reynardine down on the path.

Yvette and Jasmin looked down at the fox-fur in some surprise. It didn't look much; not very clean and not very big, a little twisted where the clumsy stitches had pulled its edges together.

'Oh dear, she's setting her doggy-poggy on us,' Jasmin said.

Yvette said, 'Ooh!' sharply, and jumped back. She had seen Reynardine lift up his head. She stared, astonished and unable to look away, as Reynardine lifted up his front end on his strange, flipper-like legs, and then got his back legs underneath him and moved himself towards them. Yvette grabbed at her sister with one hand and moved backwards.

'She's making it move,' Jasmin said.

'Yes, I am making him move,' Sarah said. She was feeling much cheerier; she almost felt like laughing. 'I can make him bite you – and I shall!'

'It's just—' Jasmin leaned forward and stooped to pick Reynardine up, but the fox-fur raised its head quickly and snapped at her. The dry little teeth made a small clacking sound. Jasmin snatched her hand away, and backed off with her sister. There was no doubt about that snapping movement of the head. Reynardine was not a puppet, was not operated by micro-chip, was not mechanical in any way. Only the heads of living things move and snap like that. Yet Reynardine wasn't like anything living they'd seen.

'Get out of my gran's garden,' Sarah repeated, and was delighted to see them obey her. They almost jumped up the bank. She did laugh out loud. After the way they'd been throwing their weight around, it was most amusing to see their frightened retreat.

They reappeared in their own yard, slithering down from the bank on to the concrete. They came to the fence and peered over nervously. Reynardine, on the path, moved round to face them. His sharp little head was tilted up, his orange glass eyes shone in the sunlight.

'What is it?' Yvette asked, and she looked at Sarah almost pleadingly, with frightened eyes.

Sarah felt pleased and strong, in control. 'His name is Reynardine,' she said reprovingly. 'He's what's called a bone-dog. My uncle made him.'

78

'But . . . it's *alive*,' Yvette said.

'Yes,' said Sarah smugly. She picked Reynardine up and, holding him, began to pick her way across the strip of garden towards the fence. 'I'll show you him,' she said kindly. Reynardine lifted up his snout and pointed it inquisitively towards the two girls. They stepped back from the fence, further into their own yard.

'Keep it away,' Yvette said shakily as Sarah reached the fence.

Sarah leaned over the fence. 'I'll let him go in your yard.'

Yvette and Jasmin both let out shrieks of fright and ran across the yard to the house. Sarah began to laugh. She shouted, as they had shouted after her, 'Scared babies, scared babies, running away!' Then she could only laugh. She could hear the two girls making noise in their kitchen, and she saw their mother's face bob close to the window, peering out to see what was in the yard that they were making such a fuss about.

Still laughing, Sarah carried Reynardine back down the path, and sat on the step of the kitchen door, stroking his dry fur. Her laughter gradually died away, but she still felt enormously pleased and happy. And very pleased with Reynardine. She kissed him and stroked him and he seemed pleased too, pushing his little snout up into her face.

'Is it Sarah?' said a voice.

She looked up and saw a tall woman standing by the fence in the other yard.

'I'm Yvette and Jasmin's mother,' the woman said. 'What have you been frightening them with?'

'Nothing,' Sarah said.

'They're very upset about something,' the woman said accusingly. 'They say you set some kind of animal on them.'

Sarah, laughing inside herself, got up and carried Reynardine over to her. 'It was this,' she said, and held the fox-fur out. Reynardine was limp now, a peculiar toy. 'My uncle made it out of an old fox-fur,' she said. 'Made it for me to play with.'

She enjoyed lying to the woman, who looked at the fox-fur with distaste. Then she looked at Sarah with suspicion. 'Well,' she said. 'I don't know why you children can't play nicely together instead of quarrelling.'

She walked stiffly back to her house. Watching her go, Sarah whispered, 'Because your children are horrible, that's why.'

Tormenting people is great fun, so long as you're not the person being tormented. Sarah had hated it when Yvette and Jasmin had made fun of her: she had cried, and had felt weak and helpless and very sorry for herself. But now that she had a means of tormenting them she didn't feel at all sorry for *them*. They deserved it, she told herself, because they had hurt her feelings. She was only paying them back for what they had done to her. But she went on and on, even when she had paid them back in full and a little over.

She watched for them to appear in their yard and

then she would go and stand where they could see her, holding Reynardine and stroking him. They could see the way he moved his head and ears, plainly no puppet or stuffed toy, and he fascinated them as much as he frightened them. They would even approach the fence cautiously, a little at a time and always ready to run back the other way, to get a better view of him.

'Do you want to play with him?' Sarah would ask kindly. 'Throw a stick for him and he'll fetch it.'

'What is it, really?' Yvette asked. 'Tell us.'

'It's a bone-dog. My uncle made it out of an old dead skin and an old dead bone.'

Their eyes glittered and seemed to roll as they widened. They didn't believe her, but they didn't have enough disbelief to dare to say anything.

'Does it bite?' Jasmin asked, and Sarah answered, 'He'll bite *you*. And his bite's deadly poison. One little bite, even if it just broke the skin, and you'd be stone dead.'

They made loud, sneering noises of disbelief and scorn, but Sarah laughed, because she could tell from their faces that they believed and that they were scared.

'I can make him do all sorts of things,' Sarah said, and put Reynardine down on the path. 'Go and fetch my comic from by the door,' she ordered grandly. The other two girls leaned over the fence and watched with taut, white faces as the strange creature hauled and scrabbled its way down the path towards the house. Reynardine could go quickly over smooth ground now, and the slight unevenness of the brick path gave him no trouble. He reached the doorstep, took a corner of the comic in his dry little mouth, and dragged it back to Sarah, who picked him up again.

'I can close my eyes and see whatever he's seeing,' Sarah said. 'I can tell him to go anywhere. I could send him into your house.'

Their eyes snapped into focus on her face. She felt full of laughter, delighted, powerful. They were listening to every word she said and they were afraid.

'Tonight,' she said. 'When it's dark and you're in bed asleep, and your mum and dad are asleep – I could send him into your house tonight, to get you.'

Yvette tried to speak but had to swallow a big lump in her throat first. Her voice was wobbly, dry and squeaky. 'It won't be able to get in. The door'll be locked and the windows.'

'That doesn't matter to Reynardine!' Sarah said. She was grinning as she spoke, with the sheer pleasure of tormenting them. 'He's *magic*! He can get through doors and windows. And he'll come creeping up the stairs . . .'

She had made her voice creepy and stealthy. The two girls shied nervously away from the fence, still staring at Reynardine as their imaginations filled with the idea of that strange, crooked little thing climbing slowly – but with menacing purpose – up their staircase in the dark.

'Our mum and dad'll stop it!' Jasmin squeaked, her last hope.

'He'll *bite* your mum and he'll *bite* your dad, and his bite's deadly poison and they'll *die!*'

Yvette put her hands over her ears and ran, and Jasmin just ran. Back into their house they went and slammed the kitchen door. Sarah stood on her garden path, holding Reynardine and stroking him, and laughed out loud. She felt a pinch on her fingers and looked down. Reynardine was biting on her fingers, as a puppy might. She pushed her hand into his mouth as she would a puppy, saying, 'Go on, bite me then, go on, go on!' And Reynardine did, quite sharply. She pulled her hand out of his mouth and was angry for a second, but then rubbed his head and laughed again before going back into the house. Puppies and kittens did scratch and nip, and there was no point in being angry.

Sarah never teased the other girls if Bryan was at home. She didn't want him to overhear, by any chance, what she was saying to them. But Bryan usually went out at some time during the day and sometimes people came to fetch him. Then she would hurry out into the yard with Reynardine, hoping to see the girls. She would even climb up on to the bank and search the patch of land to see if they were there. All time she would be full of a giggling excitement, full of anticipation of the fun she was going to have.

One lucky day she was watching from the front room window as Bryan walked away down the street, watching to make sure that he was really gone, when she saw Yvette and Jasmin's mother come out of the entry and cross the street. She was carrying a shopping bag. A surge of pure delight ran through Sarah and she jumped away from the window, hurrying through into the kitchen. Reynardine, quickly humping along the floor like a seal, was almost under her feet. At the kitchen door she picked him up, to be quicker.

She ran down the path, climbed up the bank, and scrambled down it again into the concrete yard next door. She hadn't forgotten how those two had come into her gran's garden. Neither her gran nor Bryan had been there, of course, and they had known that. They knew that their mother was always at home to defend their patch of concrete. But now their mother wasn't at home.

She was in luck. As she walked boldly across the alien concrete she heard voices from the shed. Yvette and Jasmin, chattering away. They were playing some game or another in there. Sarah changed direction and crept towards the shed. She opened the door, at the same time stopping and setting Reynardine on the floor. 'Now I've got you!' she said.

The two girls turned in surprise and then anger. They were about to speak when they stiffened and pressed back against the shed's further wall. They had seen Reynardine on the ground in front of Sarah, at the threshold of the shed.

Reynardine was small but he was uncanny, and they were very afraid of him. Even more afraid since their mother had lectured them and told them that it was impossible for an old fox-fur to move, and that they were just being hysterical. Yet here was the old fox-fur in front of them, moving like a thing alive. They felt that they had no protection from it.

'Shall I set him on you and make him bite you?' Sarah asked gleefully.

Neither of the girls made any attempt to be brave or dignified: that was most gratifying. 'No, please, please don't,' Yvette said. There was a work-table built into one side of the shed and Yvette lifted herself up on to it, to get her feet away from the danger of Reynardine's scuttling attack. Jasmin, unable to get near the bench without moving nearer to Reynardine, backed into a corner and raised her feet in the air alternately.

Sarah picked Reynardine up and made as if she would put him on the workbench, where he could easily reach Yvette. Yvette drew her legs up to her chest and folded herself into the corner behind her, whimpering. Sarah smiled and then hit on the idea of telling them how Bryan had made the bone-dog. She wasn't strictly truthful. She said that Bryan had trapped a fox and skinned it, and made great play of its having come from a *dead* fox. One of the fox's bones was sewn inside it, she said, together with the nails and hair from a *dead* man. At intervals she moved as if she would throw Reynardine at Jasmin or Yvette. Their faces were perfectly white and they were holding them in frozen, stiff positions. She'd never seen anyone so scared, not even actors on television who were supposed to be looking scared. 'And there's dead man's blood inside

85

it too,' she said, thinking that her own blood wasn't impressive enough. 'And dead man's eyes. And we put it all together at midnight – like Frankenstein. There was thunder and lightning, and the lightning made it come to life. And we put poison in it too to make its bite poisonous – a deadly cobra's venom.'

'That's stupid, then – where'd you get the cobra?' Jasmin squeaked, desperately scared and trying to defend herself.

Sarah wasn't seriously bothered by the question. 'From the Zoo. My uncle heals animals and he knows people at the Zoo.'

'Well – where – where did you get the dead man's blood and things?' Jasmin was so frightened that her words came in gasps.

'From the gallows,' Sarah said. 'From the hanged men hanging on the gallows.'

The Cornwalls were uncertain what to make of this. They didn't know what a 'gallows' was. But Yvette managed to say, 'They don't hang people anymore.' Anyway, she didn't think they did. Her tone betrayed that she wasn't absolutely certain.

Sarah glared at them both and said, with weighty conviction, 'Yes, they *do*. And we made Reynardine underneath the gallows, at midnight, in a thunder and lightning storm. And I'm gong to send him to get you one night. I'm going to send him creeping into your house in the dark and he's going to climb up on to your bed—'

Reynardine, in her arms, suddenly lifted his head high and growled.

86

Yvette and Jasmin squealed and tried to get further away, tried to push through the wall behind them. Sarah herself was so surprised and shaken that she dropped him. She had never heard him make a sound before. He hit the concrete floor of the shed with a soft, weightless thump, and wriggled himself over on to his stitched-up belly. He pointed his nose towards the entry leading into the yard from the street and growled again. Turning in the same direction Sarah heard, despite the continuing squeals of Yvette and Jasmin, the sound of feet in the entry. It wasn't Bryan's step or her gran's – it must be Yvette and Jasmin's mother.

Sarah grabbed Reynardine up from the floor and ran, away from the shed and across the yard, heading for the bank. The girls' mother appeared in the yard, carrying her shopping bags. She must have seen Sarah running away.

That evening, after the news had gone off, while Bryan was upstairs changing and her gran was watching television, there was a knock at the back door. 'Go and get that, Sarah,' Gran Gornal said.

Sarah went through into the kitchen, giving a glance at the cupboards under the sink where Reynardine was hidden. She opened the back door. Outside stood Yvette and Jasmin's mother, her arms tightly folded. She looked at Sarah coldly and said, 'I want to talk to your gran.'

Sarah went back into the front room. 'It's the woman from next door, wants to talk to you,' she said, feeling that her mouth had stiffened and wouldn't work properly.

'Oh, good God,' Gran Gornal said, heaving herself up from her chair. 'Trust her to come just when I'm getting interested.' In the blue nylon overall she wore at work, she lumbered off into the kitchen. The door swung to behind her. Sarah stood just behind it, trying to hear what was being said, but she couldn't. The voices didn't seem particularly angry.

The door was pushed open, nearly hitting her in the face. 'Sarah, come in here a minute,' her gran said.

Feeling threatened, Sarah went into the kitchen and stood by her gran. In front of her was the open door and the unfriendly woman from next door who still stood with her arms folded. 'What have you been saying to Mrs Cornwall's little girls?' Gran Gornal asked.

'*Nothing*, Gran.'

'You've been saying something to 'em.'

'I wouldn't trouble you, Mrs Gornal, but they're like I've never seen them – so nervous and jumpy, and they don't want to go to bed. Because of this animal Sarah's said she'll set on them. . . . And she's been telling them something about hanging and gallows that's really upset them. I've told them that there's no hanging these days, but I don't think they believe me. They think I'm just saying it so they won't have bad dreams – and I think they *will* have bad dreams.' Mrs Cornwall was obviously embarrassed. 'I know they're being silly, but if you could just stop your Sarah telling them these horrible stories.'

Sarah took a quick peep at her gran's face and didn't like her expression at all. It wasn't so much angry as thoughtful and considering. 'You can leave Sarah to me, Mrs Cornwall. I shall see her tells no more stories.' To Sarah she added, in a shockingly unpleasant tone, 'Get out of my sight!'

Sarah retreated into the front room, where she perched herself demurely on the edge of a chair and miserably waited for whatever would happen next.

Gran Gornal spent a long time talking to Mrs Cornwall in the kitchen. When at last she got away and came back into the front room, she was in one of her nastiest moods. She came straight over to Sarah, yanked her to her feet by one arm, and delivered a series of heavy and painfully stinging slaps to her legs. How many slaps, Sarah didn't count, but her legs glowed and smarted for an hour after.

'I'll teach you to get me in trouble with the neighbours!' Gran Gornal said. 'I'll teach you, I'll teach you!'

And when Gran Gornal was out of breath and stopped slapping, the unpleasantness went on. What was this animal she'd been telling the girls about? Where had she got that idea from? Where was that fox-fur she'd been playing with? It was almost as if Gran Gornal guessed.

'I don't know where it is. I lost it,' Sarah said, in tears. 'I lost it on the bank. Somebody pinched it.'

'You lost my fox-fur. I said it had come to its last home.'

'I just made up the stories about the animal. I was just trying to scare them.'

'Well, you succeeded, didn't you? Get out of my sight, go on – get to bed. Don't you dare come down again tonight.' As Sarah climbed the stairs, Gran Gornal was shouting, 'I'll 'phone your mother and tell her to fetch you home. I'm too old to deal with naughty kids.'

Send me home, then, send me home, Sarah whispered on her way up the stairs, but she secretly knew that Gran Gornal wouldn't. Hardly a holiday with Gran Gornal went by without something of this sort, though this was a little worse than usual.

Those tale-telling Cornwalls! If anybody deserved to be got by a deadly poisonous creeping monster, it was them. The scared babies. The spoil-sports.

Downstairs Reynardine lay in the cupboard under the sink and growled, even though Sarah wasn't thinking about him at all. At least, she didn't think she was.

Chapter Seven

Furious and sad, Sarah sat cross-legged on the bed she shared with her gran. For a long time she went over and over again how unfair it was that she had been slapped and sent to bed. Occasionally she vowed that she would get her own back on the Cornwalls, but before she could do anything, her thoughts would return to the unfairness of it all once more.

It grew later and she lay down on the bed, tired by anger. She could hear the television downstairs. She closed her eyes and saw, more clearly by the moment, the inside of the cupboard under the sink where Reynardine lay. It was dimly lit by the light coming through the slightly open door. She could see the water-pipes and a box of brillo pads.

'Come on,' she whispered. 'Open the door.'

Reynardine poked his nose and one of his paws into the gap left by the open door, and opened it as any dog or cat might. The door made a small, dull noise as it slid and scraped open. The light in the cupboard grew stronger, showing a scrubbing-brush and a plastic bowl, and a long piece of wire for unblocking the sink. The door was soon open far enough for Reynardine to wriggle out onto the floor.

He sat on the carpet and looked around. Upstairs, lying on the bed with her arms behind her head, Sarah saw exactly what Reynardine saw, with all the bright, dustless clarity of a dream. Her gran's kitchen had never looked so interesting before. She saw the expanse of carpet, and the towering cliff of the sink unit and stove. She saw the underside of the table, with all its gaunt struts and screws, which were never meant to be seen. And she saw the two doors: the door to the yard, which was shut; and the door into the front room, which was also shut. But eventually her gran would open that door to go through into the kitchen and make some tea. So Reynardine scampered over the carpet to the door of the front room, and curled himself up in the corner beside it, to wait. He couldn't close his eyes, but Sarah opened hers.

She opened them and was surprised to see the bedroom, and surprised to see it from such an angle. She felt rather muzzy and confused, as if she'd woken from a deep sleep that had lasted for hours. She left the bed and went over to the window. Looking down into the Cornwalls' concrete yard, she muttered to herself that they would be sorry, she'd make them sorry. She had nothing to do except plan revenge.

She heard the kitchen door open downstairs. Quickly, she sat herself down on the floor, leaned against the wall beneath the window, and closed her eyes. The small round window opened in the darkness behind her lids. It grew larger, and through it she saw the backs of her gran's large legs standing at the sink. Her mind was filled by the thunderous drumming of the tap's jet of water into the kettle.

Reynardine turned his head and she saw, at the end of his nose, the edge of the front room door. It was sticking out of its frame. Reynardine set his black claws into the crack and pulled, and scrabbled, pushed his nose into the slowly widening gap and thrust his head through. It was strange to see the living-room through that widening gap, and from so close to the ground. Reynardine's ears slipped through and then the whole of his slight body. Before him was the great height of an armchair's back, but he didn't stop to study. In his seal's flipper scamper, on his boneless legs, he flipped and flopped across the width of the room towards the hall and the stairs that would take him to Sarah. He had to hurry, to be hidden in the hall before Gran Gornal came out of the kitchen.

But Reynardine could move quickly on smooth surfaces such as carpets, and he was in the tiny square hall at the bottom of the stairs in a few moments. Before him was the stairs. He looked up at them, and he was so small to their steep height that he could only see the first one and, beyond that, the barest glimpse of the second.

But Sarah knew how many stairs there were and she opened her eyes in despair, blinking as she found the sight of the bedroom mismatched with her vivid Reynardine's-eye view of the stairs. She couldn't face making him climb the stairs. It would take too long. It would drive her mad.

She left the bedroom and stood at the top of the

stairs. She could see Reynardine at the bottom. She could hear her gran, still in the kitchen. Her gran's hearing wasn't of the best. Quickly, Sarah went down the stairs. She tried to be quiet, but she thought it more important to be quick. Gran Gornal wouldn't hear her from the kitchen so long as she was quick enough to be back upstairs before Gran left the kitchen. She snatched up Reynardine and began the climb back. She was almost at the top again when she heard the door between the kitchen and the front door open. It was easy enough to be quiet then, over the last few steps into the bedroom.

She sat on the bed, panting a little, more from holding her breath in excitement than from exertion. Reynardine, on her lap, held up his head and pointed his nose into her face. She bent down to him. 'You're going to go next door,' she whispered. 'Next door, and get them. Bite them, bite them!'

She carried him over to the window and opened it. Leaning over the sill she looked down into the yard. It was a long way to fall but it wouldn't *hurt* Reynardine. He wasn't alive. The only bone he had to break had already been cooked, so what harm would breaking it do him? Still, it took a while for her to nerve herself to hold Reynardine out of the window and then to drop him. Once she had, she quickly leaned over to see what had happened. She saw Reynardine on the concrete below, saw his head move as he looked about. Relieved, she threw herself on to the bed. As soon as her eyes closed, she saw through his.

Getting past the fence between the gardens was not as difficult for Reynardine as it would have been for her. Reynardine set off across the patch of garden, nosing through grass and passing under the shadow of rhubarb leaves. When he reached the chestnut-paling fence, he simply wriggled between two of the sticks. Then he was on smooth concrete in the Cornwalls' back yard, and could go quickly. He flippered across the yard to the kitchen door, which was standing open because it was a warm evening. Reynardine stopped and listened. He was looking from bright light into a much darker room, and he could see very little. But he could hear the sounds of people speaking quietly, one to another, and moving things, and shifting on their chairs. The Cornwall family were in the kitchen, eating.

Reynardine flopped down beside the kitchen step, like a badly stuffed toy that had been dropped, and prepared to wait.

But Sarah quickly got bored with waiting. The Cornwalls were eating, she thought. They wouldn't notice Reynardine slipping in, not if he was quick. And so Reynardine hauled himself up the step and poked his nose through the open door.

Seen from Reynardine's point of view, so close to the floor, the Cornwalls were terrifying giants. Up there, so high, great red mouths opening and shutting, great jaws champing, great thick forearms lifting up forks and cups. But Reynardine's head moved, looking about the kitchen. There was nowhere for him to hide, but the door into the Cornwalls' front room stood open. Reynardine made a dash for it, a flopping, flippering dash across the smooth kitchen floor and through the open door into the front room.

Behind him, a cry rose up from the dinner-table.

'What's that?'

'A cat!'

'A cat – a cat's got in, Dad!'

'A cat's just run into our front room.'

Hide! Sarah told Reynardine. Hide! They're going to come looking for you. *Hide!*

Reynardine ran to the hall, as he'd done in Gran Gornal's house, but the door was shut. So he ran and squeezed into a magazine rack instead. No real animal could have fitted in among the magazines and newspapers. He could, because he was only skin and a bone.

Reynardine's ears relayed back to Sarah the sounds of Mr Cornwall searching for the cat that had got in, moving furniture and calling, 'Puss, puss, puss!' He didn't look in the magazine rack. Back he went to the kitchen, saying, 'You must have imagined it. There's no cat.'

It was boring to keep her eyes closed, and see nothing but the black and white of the magazines that Reynardine was sharing the rack with. She could smell, too, the paper and the ink. As soon as the sounds from the kitchen were softened by the kitchen door swinging to, she set Reynardine to wriggling free of the rack. She sent him on a quick tour of the room, curious to see what the

Cornwalls had in their house. But Reynardine saw everything from below, so that it all seemed huge and distorted.

The door to the stairs was only shut to, so it wasn't difficult for Reynardine to scrabble it open far enough for his thin body to slip through. And once through into the hall, he clambered up the stairs to the bedrooms. It took all Sarah's concentration to get him up those stairs. Each separate step was a battle. Lying on her bed, she clenched her fists and her brows, gritted her teeth as she gave Reynardine the strength to climb by sheer will-power. But once he was at the top of the stairs it was so easy to move Reynardine along the landing that he almost flew. It was easy to tell which was Yvette and Jasmin's bedroom too – the one with two little beds with pink covers. Reynardine ran quickly, low to the ground and quick, across the blue carpet and disappeared beneath one of the beds.

Through his eyes, Sarah looked up at the diamond bed-springs, the rough cloth covering them, the dangling threads. She looked down at the thick dust gathered on the carpet, at comics and a lost doll's head. She lay on her gran's bed and smiled with warm satisfaction. Just wait, now! Just wait until horrible Yvette and Jasmin came to bed. They'd got her into trouble, got her sent to bed early. Just wait until they came themselves. Just wait. Just wait. . . .

Chapter Eight

It was a long time before Yvette or Jasmin came to bed. Sarah was bored with waiting. Sometimes she would hope that Gran Gornal would relent and call her downstairs again. Then she would hope not, because Reynardine would still be in the Cornwalls' house, and she would find it more difficult to control him with her gran watching her.

She would call all her concentration to the job of working up her hatred for the Cornwall sisters, gloating over how much she was going to frighten them, how Reynardine was going to jump out from under the bed and bite them . . .

She was often quite frightened of something under the bed herself. Beds always seemed to be such a handy hiding-place for monsters, and even though Reynardine was so small and didn't seem a monster to *her* – still Yvette and Jasmin were very frightened of him. She thought of how she'd feel if the wolf that she'd always dreaded was under her bed was *really* there one night, and caught her ankle in its big teeth as she climbed into bed. . . . For all she knew, Yvette and Jasmin might have relatives like Gran Gornal and Bryan, who could make it happen. . . .

She relaxed. No, they hadn't. If they had, they'd

have boasted about it. So she could set Reynardine on them quite safely; they couldn't do anything to her. She'd got into trouble for frightening them with stories, but their parents wouldn't believe that she'd actually made a stuffed toy *bite* them. In fact, *they'd* be the ones to get into trouble if they told on her. They might even be locked up for being mad. She hugged herself at the thought.

But into her pleasure, guilt came creeping. It *was* a terrible thing to do. It might even scare them to death – really, they might *die* from fright. And it would be her fault. Their mum and dad would be so sad – they might be horrible, but their mum and dad must love them, surely. There'd be a funeral, and everyone would be crying, and it would be her fault.

And what would Bryan think? Because Bryan would know, wouldn't he? He'd guess. Or he'd know by second sight. And Bryan had said that he wouldn't hurt those girls. Bryan was too kind: he only healed, he didn't hurt. Tears ran from her eyes, down the side of her head and into her ears, at the thought of her own wickedness and Bryan's goodness. He'd never want to speak to her again.

In fact, she'd better bring Reynardine back. . . . But when she closed her eyes and looked about the floor of the Cornwalls' bedroom, through Reynardine's eyes, it suddenly seemed an enormous effort. Making Reynardine climb the stairs in the Cornwalls' house had made her very tired, and now getting him to cross that bedroom floor, and go down the stairs, and creep through the front room and then through the kitchen – it was like trying to concentrate on a maths problem when you're tired and bored and just don't want to do it. Perhaps later, she thought. After all, they weren't likely to find Reynardine, and she could get him to come out of their house the next day, when she felt more like it.

She lay there on her gran's bed, and now the light was dimming and yellowing outside, and she began to feel comfortable and sleepy. Her thoughts took many odd and twisty turns, and came back again to how much she disliked Yvette and Jasmin. She forgot how guilty she'd felt about frightening them earlier. She thought of their faces, and how much she disliked their every feature and their smug expressions. Yvette's plump pink cheeks and prissy little mouth and piggy little nose. Horrible yellow hair with pink cheeks – nasty colours. And Jasmin's long bony arms and legs and aggressive eyes. She disliked the way they dressed – a kilt! She disliked the way they talked and the things they talked about. She hated their concrete yard. And she drifted off to sleep, still hating them.

But when people go to sleep, they're not switched off. They go on hearing, and they go on thinking, and the thoughts are dreams. And in her sleep Sarah still saw and heard and felt what Reynardine saw and heard and felt. She went on hating the Cornwalls – and she went on feeling guilty. And she wasn't as much in control as when she was awake.

Her dreams were of high walls, slanting inwards to

high, square ceilings. They were of the short, thick, wooden legs of dressing-tables dimpling carpets, making little hollows where dust gathered. They were of hanging edges of blankets, and trailing threads from bedcovers; of the blank, unpolished wooden undersides of dressing-tables. While she slept, Reynardine had crept from under the bed and was roaming about the room.

But he knew that he had to hide when someone came near. Hearing footsteps on the stairs, he withdrew to the furthest corner beneath the dressing-table and lay still.

Mrs Cornwall's feet, in their flat black shoes, crossed the carpet, and there was a swishing of material as she folded back the covers on the beds. Then came Jasmin's feet, in brown sandals, and Yvette's feet, in white shoes. Reynardine, in his corner, waited and half-dreamed while they undressed and were kissed and tucked in. Mrs Cornwall's feet crossed the carpet again, and the door of the bedroom closed.

Now we're shut in for the night, Reynardine thought – or was it Sarah who thought that, as she slept in the next house? Reynardine left his corner and crept forward over the carpet to the front legs of the dressing-table. Ahead of him he could see the ends of the two beds, the covers hanging down in folds. Above him he could see the tops of the beds, like cliffs – and drifting down to him he could hear the whispering of the two girls as they talked together.

Reynardine left the shelter of the dressing-table and crept forward. He was to be the wolf under the bed, the biter of ankles, the dragger into the dark.

He raised up his nose and his boneless paws, and scrabbled at the covers at the end of the bed. But the covers were smooth nylon and he could get no grip. He couldn't climb up.

He slipped under the trailing frills of the bedcover – Sarah, sleeping next door, felt the smooth, cold nylon slither over her body and shivered in her bed. Through the darkness beneath the bed Reynardine advanced, following the bed's length, towards the pillows where the girls were whispering.

He reached the place where the bedcover ended and lay there, grinning in the darkness, listening to the voices above him. The words and the voices, coiled through Sarah's dream, becoming nonsense. . . .

'Anyway, you're a blue-nosed whale,' Jasmin said.

'And you're double a blue-nosed whale with knobs on – and don't forget to polish 'em!'

'You're a blue-bottomed baboon!'

There was an explosive, spluttering noise of secret giggles above Reynardine's head.

'Blue-bellied skink!' Yvette said.

'Big ears – hey, there's something under your bed!'

'Ha! What's yellow with orange spots, got twenty legs and thirty eyes?' Yvette asked. 'I don't know either, but there's one crawling up your bed.'

'No, really!' Jasmin said. 'There really is something under your bed. I saw it move.'

'You're not going to frighten me.'

'There really *is*, Vette. Honestly, I'm not having you on, honest!'

Yvette jumped upright in bed, spilling the covers from her. 'Uur! It's not a spider, is it?'

'Bigger than that,' Jasmin said. She was edging away across her bed. 'More like . . . a rat.'

Yvette was kneeling on her bed, peering down at the floor between the beds. 'We haven't got rats,' she said in a frightened voice. The truth was, she was already thinking of Reynardine but didn't want to admit it.

'Shall I shout Dad?'

'No,' Yvette said. 'He'll say we're being stupid.' She took hold of her bed covers and pulled them up on to the bed, so that whatever was under the bed couldn't hide behind them. 'Can you see it now? What is it?'

Jasmin peered from the other side of her bed. But Reynardine had retreated further under the bed, where it was darker. 'I'm not sure. . . . There's something. . . . It might be something. . . . It's not moving.'

They looked at each other unhappily, crouched on their beds. 'We've got to find out,' Yvette said, hoping that Jasmin might volunteer to find out. But Jasmin stayed well on the further side of her bed.

'I'm going to look,' Yvette said. Slowly, she leaned towards the edge of her bed. Slowly, she poked her head over the side, her hair falling forward on to the floor. Her head hanging upside-down, she looked under the bed.

She saw an orange glow, and a white snap, and just had time to whip her face up and away as Reynardine charged from under the bed – charged to bite.

Jasmin leaped from her bed, squealing, as she saw the long shape, grey in the fading light, come flippering across the floor. 'What is it?' Jasmin yelled. 'What is it?'

Yvette was standing on her bed, screaming and jumping up and down, as if jumping would get her still further away from the thing on the floor. Jasmin jumped from her bed and made as if to run to the door, but quickly leaped back on to the bed when Reynardine scuttled towards her.

'Daddy! Daddy!' Jasmin shrieked, and Yvette, changing her mind, joined in. They screamed in panic, and from downstairs came the sound of the living-room door snapping open. Then heavy footsteps on the stairs as both their father and mother came racing up.

And Reynardine? Reynardine heard them coming and slipped quickly beneath Jasmin's bed, into the shadows where he could hide.

Mr and Mrs Cornwall threw open the bedroom door, breathless and alarmed, to see their daughters shrieking and crying, jumping up and down on their beds. Mr Cornwall was looking wildly round the room. Window was shut; no one who shouldn't be there was there; nothing was out of place. No fire, no flood, no danger.

'It's under the bed! It's under the bed!' Jasmin was shrieking. She had bounded from the bed and was clinging to her mother in the doorway. Yvette, too, came racing across the room, sobbing, to hide behind her mother and peer cautiously back into the room.

Mr Cornwall seized the end of Jasmin's bed and swung it violently away from the wall, giving a sort of skip to one side as he did so to see what, if anything, might be underneath it. 'Nothing!' he said.

'Mal,' said Mrs Cornwall, in a rather high and frightened voice. 'I think ... I think I *did* see something run under the other bed. I think there is something.'

'All right,' Mr Cornwall said, sounding frightened himself. 'All right, we'll see what it is.' And he grabbed hold of the other bed and pulled that aside too, sending it banging into Jasmin's bed. Something, some vague shape, seemed to dart away from the bed, hit the wall beneath the window, and then fall down. It lay still.

Mr Cornwall approached it carefully. He peered at it. 'Oh Mal, be careful,' Mrs Cornwall said.

'I am being careful.' He crouched down beside it, studied it, stretched out a hand to touch it, drew back ... then poked it with a finger. Then he picked it up, turned and came towards them, holding Reynardine high and upside-down by the tail.

105

Yvette and Jasmin began to howl again and to push behind their mother.

'It's nothing to be scared of,' their father said. 'Look, it's dead . . . in fact, I don't think it's been alive for years.' He held Reynardine in both hands, turned him over and over. 'It's a skin that's been sewn up.'

Mrs Cornwall was peering closer. 'It's that thing the little girl next door had! Mrs Gornal's granddaughter – that's what she was frightening them with!'

Mr Cornwall looked at his two daughters. 'Now what is going on?' he asked. 'Is this some sort of stupid game?'

'It comes alive!' Jasmin said.

'Don't be silly!'

'She said she'd set it on us!'

'Look!' Mr Cornwall shook Reynardine. 'It's just an old skin. How can it come to life?'

Yvette backed away further. She knew that Reynardine could come to life, but she wasn't going to get involved in arguing with her father about it. Jasmin, less cautious, insisted, 'Sarah's a witch! Sarah makes it come to life – she sent it to get us!'

'Oh, honestly!' Mr Cornwall said.

'I thought I saw it move,' said Mrs Cornwall.

'Now don't you start!'

'I'm just pointing out that your eyes can play you tricks,' Mrs Cornwall said. 'That girl next door has been filling their heads with all sorts of frightening stories, until they don't know what they *do* see. And now she's got that thing into our house somehow or other. I'm going to speak to Mrs Gornal again.'

'Yes, do,' Mr Cornwall said.

Turning to Yvette and Jasmin, their mother said, 'Come on, I'll put you to bed in our room.'

'I shan't sleep,' Jasmin wailed. 'It'll come after us again.'

'It won't,' said their mother. 'I shall make sure it can't.'

It was a long time before she had the girls calm enough to be able to leave them. When she came down, the fox skin was lying on the coffee table. 'Don't put it there!' she said. 'Dirty thing!'

Mr Cornwall picked Reynardine up again by the tail. 'It's not dirty,' he said. 'I think it was a fox-fur stole originally. You wouldn't mind a fox-fur on the table, would you?'

'I don't want it in the house at all,' Mrs Cornwall said. She looked at it with hatred. 'Mal, throw it outside.'

'It's dead,' Mr Cornwall said. 'It's just an old fox-fur – look.'

'Throw it outside, Malcolm,' Mrs Cornwall said firmly. 'It's a horrible thing and I'm not going to touch it, and I don't want it in this house!'

Mr Cornwall saw that there was no point in arguing about it. He shrugged, and carried the fox-fur through into the kitchen and out by the back door into the yard. His wife followed him and stood on the kitchen step.

'Throw it into their yard,' she said. 'It's their nasty thing. Let them have it.'

'I thought you were going to talk to Mrs Gornal again. How are you going to prove that the little brat was trying to frighten our two with it unless we've got it?'

'I don't care,' Mrs Cornwall said. 'Throw it into their yard.'

Mr Cornwall shrugged again, and tossed Reynardine over the fence. He fell with a thump near the Gornals' kitchen doorstep.

'You act as if you were scared of it as well,' Mr Cornwall said, as he followed his wife back inside their house.

'I'm not scared of it. I just think it's dirty. Mind you . . .' She turned to face him as they entered the living-room. 'Did you know people go next door to have their fortunes told?'

'Do they?'

'When Yvette and Jasmin told me that the little girl next door said her granny was a witch, I didn't take any notice – I thought it was just children talking. . . . But it seems that people really do think Mrs Gornal has some kind of powers. In this day and age. . . . That she's a healer or something.'

'A healer's not a witch,' Mr Cornwall said.

'What's the difference?'

'You *are* scared!'

'I'm scared of that little girl next door! What a nasty little thing she is! Who'd have thought that a child of that age would play such a trick?'

Mr Cornwall put his arms round his wife. 'It was a good one, though, wasn't it? The din our two kicked up, I thought they were being eaten by tigers! I must have gone up those stairs six at a time! And it was just some sort of stuffed toy. Whatever you say about that little girl, she must have a very persuasive tongue.'

'It's not funny,' Mrs Cornwall said. 'Not funny at all. Just wait 'til I speak to her gran.'

Chapter Nine

Reynardine lay where he'd been thrown, in the Gornals' yard, close to the kitchen step, picking up the thoughts and fears that drifted through Sarah's sleeping mind.

Though sleeping, she knew that her plan had failed. She knew that Reynardine had been discovered, and Yvette and Jasmin saved from him. She'd heard the talk of Mr and Mrs Cornwall, and what they'd called her, and even in her sleep she felt ashamed and guilty. It would serve me right, she thought, turning over ... It would serve me right if Reynardine ... And it's all Bryan's fault, she thought. If Bryan hadn't made Reynardine. . . If Bryan had given the Cornwalls headaches like I wanted him to, because he knows *how* ... It's all Bryan's fault and it would serve him right if ...

A breeze, blowing down from the bank, swung the hawthorn branches, waved the tall grasses in the garden and lifted the dry fur on Reynardine's back. Early light glinted in his orange glass eyes. All night long, through the darkness and into the strengthening light, he pushed and scrabbled at the Gornals' kitchen door, trying to get in.

It was seven o'clock when Gran Gornal opened

the kitchen door and stepped out into the yard, to peg some tea-towels and a few items of underwear on the clothesline before she went to work. She saw Reynardine, half-slumped over the step, but not in a very noticing way. Sarah had been playing with him and had left him where she'd dropped him, Mrs Gornal supposed. When she went back into the kitchen a few minutes later, she didn't notice that the fox-fur had gone. And shortly after that she let herself out of the entry-door and went to work. Behind her, in the house, Reynardine was climbing the stairs.

Upstairs, in her grandmother's bed, Sarah drifted close to waking, like a fish drifting up to the surface of a deep pool. She was hot under the covers and turned over restlessly, and her mind ran on steps . . . step after step, going up . . . every step a little struggle of lifting herself up. The steps were very large, and yet she seemed to go up them quickly and tirelessly. She didn't wake but, turning her face into the pillow, drifted deeper into sleep again.

And Reynardine went on climbing, up and up, until he reached the little rectangular landing from which the two bedrooms and the bathroom opened. He went straight to the room where Sarah was sleeping – but Gran Gornal had closed the door behind her as she'd left it that morning, and all Reynardine could do was scratch his black claws against the paint. He scratched and scratched there for a while, and would have gone on scratching, trying to get in, until the door was opened – or for ever if Sarah's sleeping mind hadn't turned on to another track. The affair of Reynardine and the Cornwalls had drifted into her sleep again, and was troublesome to her because it made her feel guilty – and so once more she was shuffling the blame on to Bryan. It was Bryan's fault. Bryan had made Reynardine when he should have known that she was only a child and couldn't be trusted. So Bryan was to blame for everything.

Reynardine left her door and crossed the landing to Bryan's room. And Bryan's door wasn't closed. It stood open slightly, quite wide enough for Reynardine to poke in his nose and push it open.

Reynardine slipped into the room and flippered across the carpet to the bed. But he couldn't climb on to the bed. It was too high. He passed under it, amongst dust and magazines, and came out again. He scrabbled at the covers which hung down, but that was all he could do.

Then the alarm clock, which stood on the floor beside the bed, blared. Bryan's hand came down from the bed above to touch the button on top of the clock and silence it. Reynardine saw, and Reynardine lay down by the clock and waited.

The clock was set on 'snooze' and, seven minutes later, it blared again. Down came Bryan's hand once more, and Reynardine set his teeth about Bryan's thumb, and bit.

Bryan was sleepy and at first only realized that something had touched him. Then, wakening somewhat, he realized that something had hurt him. He snatched his hand back to the bed. Something dragged on the thumb, and then flew off and landed with a thump on the floor, somewhere in the direction of the door.

Bryan started up on his elbow and peered across the room through his untidy hair. He saw something moving fast towards him and was unable, at first glance, to see what it was. But after screwing his eyes tight shut and opening them again he saw that it was – Reynardine.

He wasn't worried by Reynardine until he examined his thumb and saw the tooth-marks. There was even a little blood. Fuzzily, he looked down at Reynardine, who was again beside the bed, looking up, grinning and waiting. Slowly he realized that Reynardine had bitten him.

That made him sit up very sharply, pushing back the covers. Reynardine wasn't supposed to bite. What had Sarah been doing? In fact, where was Sarah? Was she up already and was this a joke? If so he'd give her what for when he caught her. He didn't think bitten thumbs very funny.

Sitting on the bed he wondered what to do. He drew in a deep breath and yelled, 'Sarah!' But there was no answer and anyway he felt stupid. He looked down at Reynardine. What was he frightened of it for? It was only a skimpy bit of an old fox-fur wrapped round a bone. He'd made it himself. It only had the strength that Sarah lent it and she was only a little girl. He wasn't going to be kept on his bed by a thing like that. He would just get up and go about his business, as he would any morning.

So he stretched out his foot to leave the bed. Reynardine leapt, Bryan snatched back his foot, and Reynardine's small, sharp, dry teeth grazed his ankle – not deeply, but painfully.

Bryan began to be angry. He wasn't one to be afraid of animals. He was used to taking a firm hand with them and didn't mind the odd scratch or nip. His hand swooped down from the bed to grab Reynardine by the scruff.

But Reynardine was cleverer than a cat, and as flexible as a bit of well-tanned fox-fur with only one bone. He twisted skilfully and got his teeth into Bryan again. And he was harder to shake off this time. Bryan was calm enough not to try and snatch his hand away, but simply keeping his hand still didn't work, as it sometimes does with a dog. Reynardine didn't let go. Hitting the fox-fur on the nose didn't work, because it wasn't hurt. Bryan had to prise open Reynardine's jaws with his other hand and he was astonished, and unnerved, to discover how strong the fox-fur had become.

'Sarah!' he said, when he was at last free of the thing and back on his bed. His hand was bleeding and it was sore. But worse than a little bite – he'd been bitten before – was the puzzlement he felt at why Sarah should want the bone-dog to bite him. What had he done that she should have it in for him so much?

He looked down at the bone-dog. It lay on his

114

carpet, propping itself up with its flipperish legs like a seal, lifting its fox-head to stare at him with its orange, glass eyes. Its narrow, triangular mouth was open, showing tiny sharp teeth, stained and wet with his blood. He suddenly saw what a horrible thing it was. He hadn't felt that about it before. He'd thought it a rather funny little thing. He'd been proud that he'd been able to make it. But now . . . The queer way it moved, so strange and so quick. The way it saw without real eyes and heard with dead ears and bit with dead teeth. . . . It really was a nasty thing. 'Sarah!' he yelled again. 'Sarah!' But Sarah didn't answer and she didn't come. His hand was beginning to drip blood on the bedclothes.

'This is stupid,' he said to Reynardine. 'You aren't going to keep me here – you needn't think you are.' He stood up on the bed, pulled the topmost blanket free – nearly unbalancing while he did it – and then threw the blanket over the fox-fur. Even before the blanket landed he had jumped from the bed, to get as close to the door as he could. He wasn't completely out of the door, and hadn't shut it properly, before Reynardine came flippering from under the blanket. He'd slipped from under it almost as easily as a sheet of paper would have done. Dashing at Bryan, Reynardine growled. Bryan had never heard the bone-dog growl before. He hadn't known that the thing *could* growl. The surprise gave him enough speed to jump on to the landing and slam the door behind him. He heard Reynardine thump into the door and begin scratching at it, tireless scratching that would go on and on, since Reynardine had one object only: to get through that door and bite Bryan again.

Bryan stood on the landing, feeling more scared and relieved than he was used to feeling, and rubbing at his hair. Then he remembered that his hand was bleeding and that he ought to do something about it. He went downstairs, angrily looking forward to having a few words with Sarah. He supposed that since Reynardine was up and about Sarah was also, and that he would probably find her in the kitchen or stretched out on the settee in the front room.

But she wasn't in either place. Maybe she was up on the bank, but he couldn't go to find her since he had only his pyjama-trousers on, and his other clothes were upstairs in his bedroom where Reynardine was waiting to bite him again. A good job it was a warm day.

He washed his bitten hand at the sink and dabbed it with a clean tea-towel soaked in cold water until it stopped bleeding. Then he opened the back door and yelled, 'Sarah!' at the bank two or three times. No Sarah came to see what he wanted. He left the door a little open, to let in the pleasantly fresh air, and put the kettle on to make himself a cup of tea. As an afterthought, he went upstairs to the bathroom and put a little diluted disinfectant on the bite. As he passed the door of his bedroom he heard the scratch, scratch, scratch still going on from the other side. It made him feel more nervous than he liked. He wondered if he was turning into a coward. But there was something very unnerving about hearing that relentless scratching, and knowing that you couldn't hurt or stop the thing that was doing the scratching, and that it wanted to bite you.

Back in the kitchen he made tea and drank it at the table, but the longer he sat there, the more glum he became. Unless he could get into his room he wouldn't be able to dress, and he'd still be in his pyjamas when his mother came home, and she'd want to know why. He tried to nerve himself to go up and deal with Reynardine. He ought to be able to. But the more he thought about it, the less he wanted to try. It was a horrible thing he'd made. Why on earth had he been stupid enough to make it? He was no Devil Gornal. He opened the back door again and yelled, 'Sarah!' But no Sarah came.

When Sarah woke, her head ached and she felt befuddled and tired. There was something bothering her, something she felt she ought to do something about, but she found it hard to think clearly about anything. It wasn't until she'd lain awake for some time, looking at the cracks in the ceiling, or at the green hawthorns through the window, that she remembered what she'd done.

She immediately felt very frightened even though she couldn't remember it all clearly. She'd sent Reynardine into the house next door – she knew that. She'd been very angry – stupidly angry. She'd sent Reynardine up the stairs and into Yvette and Jasmin's room . . . but what exactly had happened after that?

She'd meant to make Reynardine scare the two girls, bite them – but she must have fallen asleep. She didn't know what had happened. She tried to remember her dreams, but nothing was clear. She seemed to remember her name being called, but she didn't know why, or even if she'd really heard it. Oh, what if Reynardine had bitten them? What if he had killed them? The police would come, there would be terrible trouble. And the Cornwalls hadn't done anything that was really so terrible to her. When Gran Gornal and Bryan found out, they'd hate her. She sat up in her bed and cried, she felt so small and nasty and scared.

But crying calmed her a little, and she decided that she ought to try and find out what had happened. She lay down, closed her eyes, and waited and watched as that window opened in the darkness of her mind.

That opening window showed her something . . . Something like a plain of snow, seen from above. It was a little wrinkled; it shone faintly in some places, and was faintly shadowed in others. She could not imagine what it was. And there was a sound – a scratch, scratch, scratching that never stopped, and sounded like fingernails scratching on wood . . . And then there was a growl, Reynardine's growl, that she had heard only once or twice before, and it was as if the window in her mind were being squeezed shut. The strange and puzzling picture blurred and wavered and vanished altogether in the darkness behind her eyes. And though she frowned and concentrated, she could not make it open again.

She opened her eyes and waited while she became used to the ordinary sight of the bedroom again, and then she got up and dressed. There didn't seem any point in staying in bed any longer. She left the bedroom without any feeling that the day was going to be a pleasant one. Rather, she felt that something very unpleasant was bound to happen, but she couldn't be sure when it would, or exactly how unpleasant it would be.

On the landing she was stopped by the sound of scratching coming from behind Bryan's closed door. It was exactly the sound she had heard when she'd tried to find out where Reynardine was. It came from the bottom of the door, and it sounded very much like the scratching her old tabby cat had made when it wanted a door opened. Was it some animal Bryan had brought home and shut in there? She put her hand on the doorknob to open the door and find out – then she thought better of it. She went downstairs, and she could hear the scratching all the way.

She went through into the kitchen, expecting no one to be there, and was quite startled to find Bryan sitting at the table, especially as he seemed to have nothing on. 'Morning,' he said, in a tone that meant he wasn't pleased with her.

She sidled round the corner of the table and saw that he did have on a pair of the jogging-suit trousers that he wore as pyjamas. She stood by the table with her arms behind her back, and solemnly studied the dark hair growing on his arms, shoulders and chest. She thought it looked very peculiar and ugly, because the hair was so dark and his skin was so white and blue. It would have looked better if the hair had been lighter, or the skin darker. His face, too, was grown over with dark hair. She thought he looked really disgustingly scruffy and a mess.

He held his hand out to her and said, 'Look at that.' He seemed annoyed.

She looked at his hand. She thought he'd cut it at first, but when she stooped closer and had a better look she saw that he'd been bitten. She could see the little holes where the teeth had gone in. Well, Bryan had been bitten before. He'd been bitten by a snake. She couldn't understand why he seemed to be blaming her.

'What did you send it after me for?' he said. 'What have I done? I made the thing for you because you wanted it – even though I knew I shouldn't have done – and you set it on *me*!'

He must be talking about Reynardine, Sarah thought. 'Reynardine bit you?' she said.

'Oh, don't play the innocent with me! You know very well it bit me – look at me hand!'

'But Reynardine isn't here,' she said. 'I sent him next door last night, to bite them horrible two.' She would never have made such an admission of guilt to her mother, or her gran, but with Bryan there wasn't the same risk. He was usually on her side, and anyway, he'd made Reynardine in the first place.

'You sent it to bite them next door?' he said.

'Yes.' And she told him how she'd thrown Reynardine from her gran's bedroom window, how

120

she'd sent him across the garden and through the fence, how the Cornwalls had all squealed about a cat getting in when she'd sent the fox-fur dashing into their house. 'But I don't remember much after that, except for a lot of waiting. I suppose I fell asleep.'

Bryan jumped up from his chair and said, 'I ought to clout your head! *Did* you make it bite them?'

'I don't know. I told you, I fell asleep . . .'

'Well, think! You ought to know even if you were asleep. You were the one that sent it!'

Sarah tried to remember. It was like trying to remember a dream. Pictures, very bright and clear, of what Reynardine had done in the Cornwalls' house would form in her mind, but when she tried to get hold of them with words, they vanished, drifted away, sank and disappeared. All they left was a feeling of dread and unease. That feeling, and Bryan's eyes being so angry and blue, made her begin to snivel. She tried to stop but couldn't help it.

'Shut that noise! Shut it!' Bryan said. 'Look at my hand! I had to slam the door on it to keep it off me, and all my clothes are in there, so I've got to parade about like this!'

Sarah thought things through. 'Oh. Is that what that scratching noise on your door is?' Bryan didn't answer but Sarah went on thinking. She remembered trying to find out where Reynardine was that morning. She remembered the little window opening in the darkness when she closed her eyes; and the whiteness she'd seen and not understood. And the scratching noise. And then she'd heard

Reynardine growl, and the little window of sight had been squeezed shut, and wouldn't open again after that. She said, 'Uncle Bryan, do you remember telling me how we can think without knowing what we're thinking? And how bone-dogs can sort of have a life of their own after a while, because they do what we tell them to do when we don't know that we told them to do it?'

Bryan looked at her attentively.

'I think that's what Reynardine's doing,' she said, and explained about being unable to see where Reynardine was. 'I don't know how he got back in here,' she said. 'I never told him to come. And I don't know why he bit you. I didn't want him to, honest. I didn't tell him to. At least, I didn't know I did.'

Bryan sat at the table, put his head on his hands and rubbed at his face, making a rasping noise with his stubble. 'Oh, God!' he said. 'What did I do it for? Mother'll have my hide for this.'

Sarah sat on a chair, her legs dangling above the floor, and looked at her uncle sympathetically. She knew just how he felt. She said, 'Gran doesn't have to know, does she?'

Bryan looked at her, his eyes very blue, as if he thought that a particularly stupid remark.

'I mean,' Sarah said, 'the two of us could get Reynardine, couldn't we? You always say you don't mind being bitten. And I don't either – much. We could get him and hide him, and you could get dressed, and then Gran wouldn't know anything about it.'

'And what about when the Cornwalls are found, all bitten to pieces?'

'Well, we could say we don't know anything about it,' Sarah said. 'If we both say it and keep on saying it, Gran's got to believe us, hasn't she?'

'Don't bet on it,' Bryan said, but he had to admire the composed, solemn and wide-eyed stare Sarah was giving him. He couldn't have done a better imitation of untroubled innocence himself. It was what blue eyes were for. He jumped up again, but this time he wasn't angry – he was merely in a hurry to get to the stairs. 'Let's give it a go,' he said.

They hurried up the stairs, Sarah close behind Bryan and going up almost on all fours to keep up with him. But when they reached the little landing they stopped. There was no longer any noise of scratching from behind Bryan's closed door.

'What's it doing?' Bryan asked. 'Have you told it to do something different?'

'I haven't told him to do anything,' Sarah said. 'I didn't tell him to come and bite you, remember?'

'Have a look and see what it's doing.'

'I can't,' Sarah said. 'I tried this morning and I couldn't.'

'Try!'

So Sarah sat down on the top step, covered her face with her hands and tried, in the darkness inside her head, to see what Reynardine was doing. It was no good. The little round window of sight didn't open. And it felt as if she were struggling against something with her mind. As if the window not only didn't open, but was being kept from opening.

'It's no good,' she said, looking up at Bryan. 'I can't get through to him any more.'

Bryan punched the door in anger. The blow made a loud noise in the small space, and the door shook and creaked. But there was no sound from inside.

'We'll just have to go in and see what happens,' Sarah said.

'I know, I know!'

'After all, it's only a little fox-fur.'

'It hasn't bitten you,' Bryan said. But he opened the door carefully, holding on to the handle and pushing the door forward with his other hand, a centimetre at a time. He tensed to pull the door back if Reynardine showed any sign of rushing at him.

But the door opened more and more, and they still couldn't see Reynardine. Soon there was room for Sarah to duck under Bryan's arm and go into the room. She peered round the door and looked behind it, and into every corner of the room.

Bryan had come in behind her but was still clinging to the door. 'Where's it gone? Watch out for it . . .'

They waited, warily looking about them all the time. No Reynardine appeared. Bryan came further into the room, and then a little further still. The very hair on his arms seemed to bristle with alertness.

Finally assured that Reynardine was not going to attack, he moved over to the bed. His shirt and jumper lay on the floor beside it. He lifted them up, and Reynardine dashed from underneath, snapping.

'*Sarah!*' Bryan yelled. He was begging her to take control of the bone-dog, to stop it, but in the panic of the moment she couldn't even begin to think how. Reynardine made a run at her, even at her, and she jumped backwards, snatching one foot high into the air, then changing feet and lifting the other high, trying to stand and yet keep both feet in the air and away from Reynardine. The open door was behind her, and she ran through it.

She thundered down the stairs. Reynardine came tumbling lightly after her. He would have followed her into the front room except that, in a panic, she lashed out with her foot and kicked him back into the tiny hallway. Then she slammed the front room door, and Reynardine was trapped on the stairs.

But where was Bryan? Not with her. He was trapped upstairs in his bedroom. He couldn't come downstairs and she couldn't go up to join him, because Reynardine was on the stairs.

Sarah spent a miserable afternoon. At first she sat at the table in the sunny kitchen, feeling trapped and wondering what to do. Then she tried shouting to Bryan, but though she yelled until her throat hurt, she couldn't make him hear.

What she ought to do was something brave. She should open the hall door and deal with Reynardine firmly. But the way he'd dashed at her, and the thought of those dry little teeth sinking into her, made her feel that anything was better than that.

Chapter Ten

She lay on the settee in the front room and tried to see through Reynardine's eyes, but he started scratching on the hall door and she couldn't concentrate. The window behind her eyes refused to open. It was that failure which made her think she'd better do something to put Gran Gornal in a good mood. She cleared off the table, shook the cloth free of crumbs in the yard, washed up some cups, getting very wet in the process, and cleaned the sink.

It began to get near the time when Gran Gornal would come home, and Sarah rehearsed what she would do and say. Sit down, Gran, she would say. I'll put the kettle on and make you some tea. Put your feet up, Gran, and I'll run down the shop and get some pies for our tea so you don't have to cook. She began keeping a watch from the front room window, and from the kitchen window, in case her gran came through the yard.

But keeping watch did her no good. She heard voices, looked through the kitchen window, and saw her grandmother at the yard gate, talking to Mrs Cornwall.

The first shock of the sight made Sarah get as far from the window as she could, but she had to go back and look again. Climbing on the chair she'd set in front of the sink, she peered out of the window, trying to keep down so that Mrs Cornwall wouldn't see her. Gran Gornal had her back to the house. They were talking about something with great involvement – Sarah could guess what.

Then they parted and Gran Gornal turned towards the house. Sarah leapt down from the chair and ran into the front room, where she perched herself on the edge of the settee, as if she'd been sitting there all day.

She heard the kitchen door open and close. Gran Gornal's voice called, 'Sarah!' She thought about answering, but then decided not to. 'Bryan!' Gran Gornal shouted. She didn't *sound* angry.

The door from the kitchen opened and Gran Gornal came through. She paused when she saw Sarah. Then, slowly, Gran Gornal's fists went up to her hips and lodged there. She said, 'I'm going to ask you one question, my lady. Where is it?'

Sarah knew that whatever she said, trouble would follow. She knew that the worst thing she could say would be, 'Where's what?' So she swung her legs and said nothing.

Gran Gornal came across the room, her hands still on her hips. 'Where's the thing you set on the Cornwalls? I know there's something . . . I've known there's been something going on for days, but I didn't say anything. I thought you had enough sense – but I was mistook in that!' She stopped short, and stared at the door into the hall. From behind it, still, came the sound of scratching. 'What's that?'

Sarah knew that the game was up and that she had better confess quickly, but she couldn't think of the right words. Gran Gornal impatiently reached out to open the door. Sarah bounced off the settee. 'Don't open the door, Gran!'

Gran Gornal's hands went back to her hips. 'Why shouldn't I open my own door?'

'Because he'll bite you.'

'Who'll bite me?'

'Reynardine,' Sarah said, and added, 'The bonedog.'

There was a pause. The next thing Gran Gornal said was, 'Where's Bryan?'

'He's upstairs – Reynardine bit him. Reynardine's in the hall, and I'm stuck down here and Bryan's stuck up there. I've tried to make Reynardine behave but I can't do it any more, Gran!'

'*You've* tried to make him behave?' Gran Gornal said.

'Uncle Bryan put my blood in it,' Sarah explained.

Gran Gornal tipped her head back slightly and said, 'Ah.' She seemed quite calm and good-tempered, but Sarah knew well enough that she was plotting revenge and retaliation. Lowering her head and looking squarely at Sarah, Gran Gornal said, 'I'm going to open that door. And if that thing so much as nips me you're in for it, Sarah White. Do you hear me?'

And Gran Gornal went over to the door.

Sarah felt her whole body turning stiff and cold. She was staring at the door without being able to look away. Her gran was going to open that door in a moment, and then Reynardine would bite her, as he'd bitten Bryan, and then she, Sarah, would get the blame. It wasn't just that she'd get smacked: it was a horrified feeling that the worst thing that could happen was that she should bite her gran – no, that Reynardine should bite her gran. It would be so unfair, so wrong. It hadn't been Gran's fault . . .

Gran Gornal opened the door. She stopped and picked up Reynardine. He hung from her hand, limp and unmoving. 'My fox-fur,' Gran said, and glared at Sarah. 'I thought you was playing a lot with it. I should have known.' She lifted up her head, filled her lungs and yelled, in a voice so loud it made Sarah jump, 'Bryan Gornal! Get down here!'

They heard a door open upstairs and then Bryan came down, fully dressed now. Gran Gornal shoved the fox-fur at him and he shied away. Reynardine fell to the floor. Only his snout moved a little.

'Now you can get on and unpick that,' Gran Gornal said.

Sarah couldn't believe what had been said for a moment. She saw Bryan reluctantly pick the fox-fur up and stand holding it, and heard her gran repeat the order to unpick it.

'No!' she said. 'Gran, no, please – don't do that.'

'You shut up,' Gran Gornal said. 'Don't you speak to me. And as for you,' she said to Bryan, 'what you were thinking of, to make such a thing and give it to a child, I don't know. Now you can get on and take it apart.'

'It bit me,' Bryan said, in a bid for sympathy.

'Good,' his mother said. 'I only wish it was poisonous, like you've been telling them little girls next door. Come on – get in there, get a knife, and take it apart.'

'No!' Sarah yelled. She caught hold of her gran's arm. 'Don't kill him, please don't. I'm sorry, I won't do it again! I promise, I promise!'

Her gran pushed her away, so that she went stumbling back and fell on to the settee. Bryan gave her what she thought a cowardly look, and went through into the kitchen. Gran Gornal followed him and shut the door.

In tears, in a rage, Sarah got up and ran across the room, crashing into the closed kitchen door. She pulled it open and pushed past her gran, who was standing just behind it. Then she could see Bryan, standing by the sink, holding Reynardine. There was a long, sharp knife in his hand, and he was pushing the blade under the string stitches that held Reynardine together and cutting them through.

'Bite him!' Sarah yelled. 'Bite him, Reynardine! Bite him!'

But Reynardine did nothing. As each stitch was cut, the fox-fur sagged a little more. And she was too angry, her fury and her grief too undirected, to have any effect.

Gran Gornal had hold of her and hustled her into the front room, shoved her down on the settee. 'Bite him? I'll give you bite him – I'll give you a good hiding in a minute, my girl!'

'You're horrible!' Sarah shouted, slapping at her. 'You're a murderer and I hate you. I wish he'd bitten you – I want to kill you!'

'Yes,' Gran Gornal said, folding her arms. 'I know you do. That's why that thing's got to be taken off you.'

Sarah jumped up from the settee and ran into the kitchen again. She was too late. Reynardine lay on the table, all unstitched, nothing but a fox-fur again. Bryan was at the sink, running water over the things from inside Reynardine: a bone, a ball of plasticine, containing her nail and hair clippings. She ran over and punched him in the back. He turned away from her, hunching his shoulders defensively, but made no attempt to stop her hitting him. 'It's for the best, bab,' he said. 'I never should have made it.'

Her gran pulled her away from Bryan, saying, 'That's it. No more. I don't see why I should put up with this. I shall 'phone your mother tonight, Madam, and tell her to come and fetch you tomorrow.' Pushing Sarah into a corner, she said, 'You're spiteful and spoilt, my girl. As for you,' she shouted at Bryan, 'you can put that fox-fur back in my wardrobe and I'll thank you to keep your hands off my things in future!'

It was an awful evening. Gran Gornal made Sarah sit on the settee in the front room, told her to stay

131

there and not to move or else, and then went out to the house of a friend who had a telephone. Bryan came downstairs while Gran was still out, but he was too embarrassed to say anything. He sat in an armchair and looked miserable.

'Traitor!' Sarah whispered at him. 'Cheat! Liar!' He was everything bad. 'Murderer. I hate you and I shall never speak to you again.' He didn't bother to answer.

Gran Gornal was a long time away. When she did come back she was just as angry as before, but in a quieter way. 'Don't think I'm going to start cooking for you pair,' she said, slamming the door behind her. 'You can starve for all I care. And you, Madam, can get upstairs and find your things. Bring 'em down here for when your mother comes tomorrow.'

'You've really rung her, then?' Bryan said.

'Where d'you think I've been all this time? I've told her mother I don't want to see her again if this is the way her's going to behave.'

Sarah went upstairs rather than listen to any more of this. She pulled her suitcase from under the bed, opened it, and began stuffing her clothes inside, not bothering to try and fold them. Halfway through the task she went to the wardrobe and looked inside. She could just see Reynardine's nose, hanging down from the rail his empty skin was slung over. Tears came into her eyes as she thought how wicked it was, how wicked, wicked, to stop him living just because of something she'd done. It hadn't been Reynardine's fault that the Cornwall girls had been frightened. It hadn't been Bryan's fault either, if she was honest. It had been her fault, all her fault.

She was so overcome with guilt and sorrow that she couldn't stand. She sat on the floor in front of the open wardrobe and cried.

Downstairs Bryan said awkwardly to his mother, 'She was very good, you know.'

'Don't you speak to me.'

'Oh, come on, Mother. The girls next door had been teasing her and she's only little. She just wanted to get 'em back. If I hadn't made her the bone-dog there'd just have been a lot of slanging over the fence, and you wouldn't have thought any the worse of her for that.'

'I know how much you're to blame – there's no need to remind me.'

'Yes, I am to blame,' Bryan said. 'More than Sarah. I should have known better. But I didn't think she'd be so good with it. That's the point. How was I to know that she'd be able to send it into next door and make it bite people? I mean, I know she could make it toddle round while it was right in front of her, but if I'd known she'd be able to send it right out of sight, and growl and whatnot, I never would have made it, honest.' He looked at his mother, who seemed to be taking a sly interest in what he was saying, despite her pretence that she wasn't listening at all. 'I didn't think any kid of her age could be that good,' he said.

There was a short silence before Gran Gornal said,

'You shut up. You've done enough. I don't want to hear any more from you.'

Upstairs, Sarah had stopped crying. She was still sitting on the floor, looking up at Reynardine dangling in the wardrobe. She was thinking that if he was made once, he could be made again. It hadn't seemed that difficult: a bone, some nails, some hair, a drop of blood. She felt that something about the process of making a bone-dog was escaping her . . . it couldn't be that simple, could it? Still, Bryan knew. She'd get it out of him. She might have to go home tomorrow, but all the fuss would be forgotten by next year and, knowing her gran, Reynardine would still be hanging in the wardrobe, even after all that time. She wondered what it felt like to be unstitched and taken apart . . . but hanging upside down in the wardrobe like that must be like a deep, deep sleep. The year would go quickly for Reynardine. When she put in his bone again, next year, and sewed him up, he wouldn't know that anything had happened. Just you wait, Grandmother Gornal, until next year when . . . But she hastily turned her thoughts away from that sort of thing. That was just the kind of thinking that had got her into such trouble, and had ended in Reynardine being unstitched when it hadn't been his fault at all.

No, she promised herself and Reynardine, next year I won't do anything stupid. You'll be a pet – just a pet. One that doesn't need feeding or brushing or taking to the vet's. And one that doesn't bite.

*

The rest of that evening was so unhappy that Sarah woke the next day glad that her mother was coming to fetch her. No doubt she was going to be in disgrace with her mother too, but at least it would be a change from her gran's angry stares and angry silences.

Gran Gornal had taken the day off work in order to be in when her daughter arrived, which didn't improve her temper. And when Mrs White did arrive, looking hot and bothered from the train and the bus, Gran Gornal said, 'Go outside and play for a bit, Sarah. And keep out of trouble or I'll give you what for.'

Sarah went up the garden and sat on the bank under the hawthorn trees. May blossom still decorated them, but she took no pleasure in it that day. She was tired of Gran Gornal's, and the bank, and the may; now she was impatient to be home. She could see the Cornwall girls in their yard, but she no longer wanted to torment them. That had caused too much trouble. And they, though they saw her, kept well away. It seemed to Sarah that the trees of the bank and the scrubby plants of her gran's garden were all sulking, and she would be glad to be rid of such sullen company.

She went back to the house a couple of times to see if she and her mother could go yet, but her mother and her gran were still talking and she was sent off again. The second time they sent her away she just sat down on the red-brick kitchen step. The door was pushed slightly open by her back, and she could hear her gran's voice saying, 'I don't care, Sheila. I don't care what her dad believes or don't believe. Her's a Gornal, and if you don't teach her how to use it, then it'll use her.'

Her mother sighed and said, 'Oh, I dunno . . .'

'I do,' said her gran. 'Her can come back here again next year, and then I'll show her a thing or two – but don't you spoil her! Little Madam!'

So I'm a Gornal, am I? Sarah thought. Even though my name is White. Well, look what I made Reynardine do. She sat looking over the garden and felt a warm pride spreading through her. And I could have made him do better things, she thought. She wasn't sure what, but there had to be something more worthwhile than frightening the girls next door . . . Healing, she thought. Gran Gornal heals, Bryan heals. If I'm a Gornal I must be able to heal too.

Her eyes hazily filled with the green of the hawthorn leaves and the white of the last may blossom as she sat considering it. Bryan and Gran healed by stroking . . . well, suppose someone had a pain, a headache . . . and suppose she started stroking their forehead. It would be like sending Reynardine off somewhere: she'd have to concentrate on sending the pain away. She wondered if she could. She'd have to try. She hoped someone would get a pain, soon.

HAUNTINGS

Susan Price

'Why?' I said. 'Why does she come back?'
Gran said: 'Why was her murdered, poor wench?'
Take it from me, that's what they're like, real
hauntings. All it takes to bring you to your knees
in suffocating fear is the sound of walking and the
jingle of a bunch of keys.

Ten terrifying hauntings that will linger in your
mind long after, that will make you glance over your
shoulder, that will fill you with delicious unease . . .
These are some of the best ghost stories you will
ever read.

Another Hodder Children's book

NIGHTCOMERS

Susan Price

Last night I dreamed that I saw him crawling towards me on his hands and knees, though his eyes stared through me, as if he would crawl through me – and I woke in a cold horror that I could not explain and cannot forget . . .

A graveside lament, a stolen kiss, a lover's revenge, a mourner mute with grief . . .

Nine nerve-tingling night-time visitations to freeze your body and haunt your mind – an unforgettable collection of ghost stories by the author of the Carnegie Medal-winning *Ghost Drum*.

Another Hodder Children's book

THE STORY COLLECTOR

Susan Price

'Elsie, do you know any other stories?'
'Stories, Master?'
'Yes, you were telling one the other day in the kitchen, about a woman and the Devil.'
Elsie, with a thrill, sat down on one of the big polished chairs.
Mr Grimsby sat back in his chair and lifted his glass.
'Do begin.'
'Well, Master, it was like this . . .' Elsie said.

And so the Story Collector gathers his stories, from housemaids and soldiers, from dogs and the dying – tales of all kinds and about all things. There's a tale of a dancing shilling, a soldier who died too soon, three husbands humiliated, a stingy old man, a king subdued and a dog who told lies . . .

ORDER FORM

0 340 68331 7	THE GRAVE-DIGGER *Hugh Scott*	£3.99	❑
0 340 65572 0	OWL LIGHT *Maggie Pearson*	£3.99	❑
0 340 68076 8	NIGHT PEOPLE *Maggie Pearson*	£3.99	❑
0 340 69371 1	THE BLOODING *Patricia Windsor*	£3.99	❑
0 340 68300 7	COMPANIONS OF THE NIGHT *Vivian Vande Velde*	£3.99	❑
0 340 68656 1	LOOK FOR ME BY MOONLIGHT *Mary Downing Hahn*	£3.99	❑
0 340 62655 0	HAUNTINGS *Susan Price*	£3.99	❑
0 340 65605 0	NIGHTCOMERS *Susan Price*	£3.99	❑
0 340 70902 2	THE STORY COLLECTOR *Susan Price*	£3.99	❑

All Hodder Children's books are available at your local bookshop or newsagent, or can be ordered direct from the publisher. Just tick the titles you want and fill in the form below. Prices and availability subject to change without notice.

Hodder Children's Books, Cash Sales Department, Bookpoint, 39 Milton Park, Abingdon, OXON, OX14 4TD, UK. If you have a credit card you may order by telephone – (01235) 400414.

Please enclose a cheque or postal order made payable to Bookpoint Ltd to the value of the cover price and allow the following for postage and packing:
UK & BFPO – £1.00 for the first book, 50p for the second book, and 30p for each additional book ordered up to a maximum charge of £3.00.
OVERSEAS & EIRE – £2.00 for the first book, £1.00 for the second book, and 50p for each additional book.

Name..

Address..

....

....

If you would prefer to pay by credit card, please complete:
Please debit my Visa/Access/Diner's Card/American Express (delete as applicable) card no:

Signature..

ExpiryDate...